DECEPTION & DESIRE

AN ARRANGED MARRIAGE ROMANCE

SIERRA VOSS

Copyright © 2025 by Sierra Voss
All rights reserved.
No part of this book may be reproduced in any form or by any electronic or mechanical means, including information storage and retrieval systems, without written permission from the author, except for the use of brief quotations in a book review.

many words. He's the kind of man who'd rather send an envelope of unmarked bills to my apartment when I'm low on rent than have a genuine conversation about emotions.

Something is wrong. Something is very, very wrong.

I grab his hand. "*Papà*. What's going on?"

He squeezes my hand back. "Come. I'll explain when we're inside."

"Is this about the Guild?" I ask anyway as he leads us in. "Are you in danger? Do you need me to get you out?"

My father laughs humorlessly as he pushes through the doors, bypassing the main reception area altogether to beeline for a set of doors on the far side of the hall.

"You worry about me too much."

"I feel like I worry about you an adequate amount, actually," I snap back at him before glancing back over my shoulder. "I think the restaurant was back there."

He ignores me and continues to pull me across the hall.

I dig my heels in and pull us to a stop. "Not another step until you give me *something*. Where are you taking me?"

"There's a room set up in the back. It's...more discreet."

Something finally clicks.

"Who else is here?"

"Mia..."

"No," I take a step back. "Tell me."

"I can't—"

"Can't or won't? Because if this is another one of Teo's fucking interventions to get me to join the Guild, I'm leaving right now."

"Mia!" My father's voice booms out loudly enough for several of the other guests to look our way. "You will take my hand, and you will follow me into that room, or else, I swear to God, I will drag you in there myself."

I snort. "Good luck with that. We both know your back isn't up to it."

"This is not a game anymore." Each word that leaves his mouth feels like ice slicing across my skin. "You know how precarious the situation is between the Guild and the Prince's Hand right now."

"Is this some kind of test?" I hiss back. "Because if it is, then I wouldn't know a thing about any of that, would I?"

"We need this alliance—"

"*We?* I have nothing to do with this."

"Amos Rubio would disagree. You're my *daughter*."

Something stirs within me at the mention of the Cartel's kingpin—the man responsible for so many of my father's gray hairs and the eternal thorn in the Guild's side.

As much as I loathe having to admit it, my father has a point. If the Cartel targets Marco Chiavari, his entire family is at risk by association. And, from what I've gathered so far, an alliance with the Prince's Hand is our best bet to ensure that never happens.

But the Guild's Italian contemporaries from Manhattan have been feuding with them for years. So it's no real surprise that negotiations aren't going smoothly.

Despite the fact that Teo married the don's sister.

"Give me one honest reason I should follow you into that room." I glare at my father.

He matches my glare, our bright green eyes clashing.

"I will die if you don't."

Right. This all suddenly becomes very simple.

It's almost alarming how quickly my body relaxes, how I slip my hand back into my father's and follow him to whatever awaits me behind those doors.

"I'm sorry," he whispers before pushing them open.

The room is smaller than I expected, beautifully decorated and cast in flatteringly warm lighting courtesy of a small chandelier hanging from the ceiling. Chairs flank each side of the room, facing forward toward the far wall where...five sets of eyes turn to face us.

Three I recognize immediately, having known them for my whole life. There's another person I don't know at all, but I can guess from his dog collar why he's here.

And then there's the other person.

Yeah. I recognize him, too.

Tall and broad, looming in the center of the room with an expression of carefully crafted composure. His dirty blonde hair is pulled away from his face. It accentuates the tightness of his jaw—the only giveaway that he'd rather be anywhere else.

Had he loomed like this the last time I saw him? Had he gazed at me with those piercing brown eyes? He certainly hadn't been wearing a suit that time, not one that hugged every curve of his muscles so tightly he might rip the seams if he flexed his muscles.

All I remember was that he was going to attack Teo. I'd acted on instinct, taking him down, the same way I'd done with that drunk bastard at the VIP table.

Now, he was standing before me—my final destination, apparently.

The don of the Prince's Guild, Leon Natali.

This isn't a dinner. It's not even an intervention.

It's a wedding.

2

LEON

Of course, it would be her.

Her.

Of course.

Because when has anything in my life gone entirely to plan?

"You're marrying me off to *him?*" Mia hisses to her father, but she makes no effort to prevent the rest of us from hearing.

Out of the corner of my eye, I see Teo flinch. The Guild's don has never seemed particularly thrilled by the arrangement either, but he's somehow convinced Marco of its merits.

Enough for Marco to bring his daughter here personally —a feat I'm sure is impressive, but one I decidedly don't care enough to ask about. I'm only here for one thing. Everything else is Teo's mess to sort out.

But it's Cassandra Moretti who speaks up first. "Mia, please."

The redhead turns on the woman in anger. "You *knew* about this?"

"I tried to warn you! You never picked up the phone."

"You could have come to *Candelabra* at any point."

"She couldn't." Teo throws Cassandra a tired look. "She shouldn't have tried to contact you at all."

Cassandra folds her arms across her chest, a strikingly formidable creature despite the softness of her features. "She's my best friend. I wasn't going to let her get married without me."

Teo sighs, gesturing to the man next to her. "Rocco, we really need to have a conversation about confidentiality."

The heavily tattooed ex-don throws an arm around his wife's shoulders and shoots Teo a lazy smile. "I'm retired, remember? I don't answer to you."

"You're on sabbatical."

The two continue to bicker about semantics, but my attention is quickly recaptured by the woman before me.

If it weren't for the fact her eyes were darting around so quickly, I would have sworn she'd frozen entirely in shock.

They hadn't told her. They'd dressed her up like *that* and dragged her to this hotel without so much as a heads-up. There was a part of me that would have probably felt sorry for her if I weren't in an equally dire position.

As if sensing my gaze, Mia Chiavari finally lets her eyes rest on me again.

"Why? Why you?"

For a moment, it's hard to look away from the open vulnerability on her face.

She is beautiful. But that much I knew already; it was an objective reality that one tended not to forget.

The clothes she wore only accentuated that fact. The

shade of her dress perfectly complemented her slightly bronzed skin. Her fiery hair—cascading over her shoulders in subtle waves—drew the eye away from her generous cleavage to where it softly framed her face.

Mia Chiavari was objectively beautiful, but it was her expression that drew me in.

I liked the stubborn set of her jaw, the determination in her alarmingly bright, emerald-green eyes. I even liked the measured elevation of her brow as she assessed and reassessed her environment. She took the measure of me, like she was plotting five separate ways to kill me.

She was a fighter. And *that* was what set my heart to racing.

"Natali is in need of an heir, Mia—" Teo begins to answer for me, only for Mia to cut him off.

"I wasn't fucking talking to you."

My eyebrows raise at that. The don of the Guild doing as he was told is new. Everything about her spiritedness calls to me like a siren song.

"Honey." This time, it's Marco who speaks. The older man holds onto her arm more firmly. "This is the last step in securing the alliance. He will ensure your safety as long as you provide him with a child."

Mia suddenly looks very close to vomiting. "You're *selling* me to him."

"This is not a negotiation."

The two of them stare at each other for a moment as something wordless passes between them. Then, Mia swallows hard and takes a step back.

"What kind of choice is this?" she whispers.

I half expect her to start crying, but she simply stares at her father with a grief I'm not sure how to comprehend.

Somehow, it's so much more terrible because she *isn't* crying. Everything about her declares that her heart is breaking right before my eyes, but she doesn't shed a single tear.

Perhaps my reaction is more to do with my relationship with my own parents, but surely, this is not a normal reaction to being told such a terrible thing.

"I'm sorry," Marco whispers back. "I love you."

I have to look away for a moment, forcing my mind to focus on all the reasons I need to do this.

Ever since my mother died...ever since I *killed* my mother for threatening the life of my sister...the Prince's Hand has been in freefall.

I have no second. I have no heir. There's no one left to pick up the pieces if I die. And there's a strong likelihood of that happening, considering the war with the Cartel on the horizon.

The prospect of dying has never been of particular significance to me until now.

Now, my potential death has become quite an inconvenience.

Winning this war is dependent on an alliance between the two Italian factions. An alliance I am willing to consider for the sake of my sister, who decided to endanger herself once more by marrying the don of the Guild.

Then again, I'd be willing to consider *anything* if it kept her and my niece safe.

They're the only family I have left in the world.

"And you're okay with this arrangement, are you?" Mia yells at me, emerald eyes screaming louder than her voice ever could.

The Guild needs my support, but they're worthless

without me. I'm a risk. If I die at the wrong moment, it could endanger everyone else.

They need an insurance policy—an heir to my throne—as soon as possible.

A wife was the simplest solution.

And if it meant the alliance would become viable...if it kept my sister safe...

"Yes."

It's the first words I've spoken out loud to her since that fateful day all those months ago.

I thought she was nothing more than Teo's feral bodyguard. Entirely too sure of herself, judgmental, mindlessly loyal. Though her little party trick of toppling men three times her size was, in fairness, a useful one.

Thinking about it now, of course, it would make sense that she was Marco Chiavari's daughter.

The oldest surviving member of the Guild was perhaps the most respected man at the negotiation table. When he made me the proposal, it had felt like something akin to an honor.

At least *this* I could get right. I could marry a respected woman. I could sire an heir. I could save my family.

But all my plans will fall to the wayside if Mia doesn't make it down the aisle.

"You're okay with marrying a total stranger, so that, what? You can knock her up at your earliest convenience? Force her to bear you an heir she doesn't want? Own her like some kind of...dairy cow?"

Mia storms forward relentlessly, leaving her father behind.

"Yes," I inform her. "This union will save lives."

She comes to a stop right in front of me, long hair

tipping down her back so that she can look me in the eye. "This union might kill *me,* not that any of you bastards give a shit about me."

"It is as your father said. I will keep you safe."

"That's not what I meant."

I can see the resentment in her gaze, all her pain bubbling to the surface of her expression.

I'm taking away her future. All her plans, her goals, her dreams, ruined by the monster who is the don of Manhattan. In her eyes, I was her greatest adversary, the enemy she would have to whore herself out to for the greater good.

Once, it might have pained me to be perceived like this.

But these days, I don't have much time for sentimentality.

"I will not force you to marry me. You can walk out that door right now, and I will not let a single person come after you," I tell her truthfully, ignoring the way Teo and Rocco seem to bristle at my words.

Mia swallows again, her gaze beginning to waver.

"But you know what the consequences will be if you do that." I keep hold of her gaze. "It's your choice."

She manages to fight through a few more seconds of rage, before closing her eyes completely. She's simply breathing in and out, gathering herself now.

She doesn't open her eyes when she speaks again. "If I do this, know that I will never forgive you. I will despise you until the day I die."

"I can live with that."

"I will never love you, either." Her eyes flash open. "And I will not tolerate any mistresses."

"Nor will I tolerate any man who looks at you with anything less than respect," I counter easily. That part, at least, is something that has always come naturally to me. I take care of my things.

She gives me a disbelieving look. "So you're just fine with us condemning each other to celibacy?"

I take a moment to rake my eyes very purposefully over her body. The curve of her hip, the toned muscles of her arms, the expanse of her bare neck. The attraction comes naturally, too. "Not quite."

A pretty little flush spreads across her cheeks. "Beyond what is necessary to get me pregnant," she amends bitterly.

So, she is not completely adverse to the sight of me then. Interesting.

"I've made my decision, Miss Chiavari. As I've said, the choice is yours."

Mia glances back at her father, who has now made it down the aisle to hover nervously at her elbow.

They share another long look that I pointedly stare away from. I notice, for the first time since Mia entered the room, the priest standing at my side, silently taking in the entire situation.

I dread to think what Teo must be paying him for this.

Mia suddenly clears her throat, drawing my attention back to her. Her chin is now stubbornly pointing in the air.

"I will marry you," she declares solemnly, and my heart begins to race in my chest.

This is truly happening.

"I will fulfill my duty to the Guild and to my father, and that is all," she continues before turning to look at Teo. "I assume this means I'm no longer considered a liability?"

There's a bitterness in her tone that I don't quite understand, but I watch as Teo nods. "Once you become a Natali, your allegiance will be to the Prince's Hand."

Mia chokes on a laugh. "So, I'm someone else's problem now, am I, *Princeling?*"

"Mia," Cas says quietly.

"I'm so furious at all of you," her friend snaps back.

Cassandra seems to accept this. "I know. I wish it was different. I wish we could have planned this together. You can hate me. That's okay. All I can do is be here for you now."

If I weren't standing so close to her, I might not have picked up on the fact that Mia's hands begin to shake.

She quickly balls them into fists and turns sharply to the priest. "Just get on with it."

The last wedding I attended was my sister's. Isabella had flown me out to Vegas for what was supposed to be a weeklong trip. I made it through the vows before turning right back around and heading straight home to New York.

This is somehow worse.

I couldn't have stopped Isabella if I'd tried. She was in love, and to her, that was worth all the risk that came with it.

Whatever this sham of a marriage will turn out to be, there's no way to sugarcoat it by blaming love. It's a transaction, a soulless binding of souls in the presence of four entire witnesses.

Every word that comes out of the priest's mouth feels like a death sentence.

The only person in the room that might feel worse is the woman before me. Which is somehow oddly comforting.

"Leon Natali and Mia Chiavari, have you come here today to enter into this covenant of marriage freely and without reservation?" the priest asks.

I feel the corner of my mouth twitch at the sight of Mia rolling her eyes. "Oh, yes, no reservations here."

When the priest looks at me for my confirmation, I simply nod—I don't trust myself to speak.

He instructs me next to take her hand, which would be easier if she wasn't still gripping her fists together. But eventually, I manage to coerce her fingers flat against my palm while desperately trying to ignore the small tremors running through them as they are pressed against my skin.

The ceremony continues with us both monotonously repeating his words verbatim. It's Marco who supplies us with rings, simple bands that complement the color of Mia's dress.

I barely register the coolness of the metal as Mia slips the ring on my finger. I'm more focused on the way her fingers wrap around my wrist to hold it steady, as if she doesn't trust me not to jerk my hand away.

When it's done, we both look away from our hands at the same time and I'm suddenly very aware of how close she is, of how soft her fingers feel in mine.

"Leon, you may now kiss your bride."

I don't really think when I bring her hand up to my lips. But I'm rewarded with an unguarded moment of surprise as I press a kiss across her knuckles.

"May I present to you, for the first time, Mr. and Mrs. Natali."

3

MIA

There is a heat in Leon's eyes as he kisses my hand, that makes me momentarily breathless.

For a man who has only exhibited the iciest of demeanors since the moment I stepped into the room, this sudden shift is alarming.

It's not fair, really. This would all be a lot more bearable if I could draw a very clear line under any physical attraction I felt for him. That way, I'd know for sure if I was acting out of duty as opposed to anything else.

Because logically, I know this man to be soulless, dangerous, and, quite frankly, controlling. I hadn't missed how easily he'd spouted that nonsense about not tolerating male attention.

For that reason alone, I yank my hand from his grasp at the earliest opportunity.

But, objectively speaking, Leon Natali wasn't the worst thing I could be looking at right now.

Which makes things a little blurry.

Leon Natali is confusing me with his stupidly intense

eyes and gentle touches and his perfectly indecent scent of rum spice and black pepper.

My husband, ladies and gentlemen, I think sarcastically, having to prevent myself from rolling my eyes. What a sham.

"Congratulations," my father whispers as he goes to kiss my cheek.

I let him, if only for the reassurance that he was still alive and that my decision to marry a mafia don was entirely warranted.

The thing is, there are only two people who would have the power to threaten my father's life like that.

Fortunately for me, they're both in this very room.

I turn on Teo Vitale in an instant. "There. Now I'm no longer a thorn in the Guild's side. I hope you don't mind taking a walk with me off the edge of Brooklyn fucking Bridge."

"It was out of my hands, Mia." The Guild's don throws his hands up defensively. "I warned you this might happen if you didn't join us formally."

"Did I miss a memo? Last I heard, you wanted me to run a casino, not marry your brother-in-law!" I snap right back.

I can feel Leon shifting behind me, clearly growing impatient, but I stubbornly ignore him.

"Where is it you get off, Vitale? Pretending to be my friend, offering me a way out only to pull the rug out from under me? Not a word from you in months, and now this?" I begin to step forward. "I thought we had an understanding, but to *threaten* my fucking—"

A hand wraps around my forearm, preventing me from throwing myself forward to strangle Teo with my bare hands.

"I think we're all a bit tired of this blame game," Leon's

voice is in my ear, low and bored. His breath against my neck makes me shudder involuntarily. "I have places to be."

I try to pull my arm from his grasp and fail spectacularly. "Then *leave,*" I huff back at him.

"Not without you."

I grimace. "Okay, so you put a ring on my finger, and suddenly I'm your property?"

"Technically, yes." He sneers down at me in a way that makes me think he's only saying it to get under my skin. Successfully, I should add. "But in this instance, we have unfinished business."

I show him my ring finger as if it were my middle finger. "I think our business is concluded."

He looks away, suddenly looking slightly put out as he examines the chandelier above us quite extensively.

But before I can question it, Cas approaches, pulling me into a half-unwilling hug.

There, with her lips close to my ear, she whispers, "You have to consummate the marriage."

Oh.

Fuck.

Leon takes a very purposeful step away from my father.

I knew, logically, that this would have to happen eventually, what with the demand on this marriage being to solely produce heirs. But I'd been relying on the idea that I'd have weeks to prepare (and get very, very drunk) to maintain my sanity during all of this.

Now that safety net was being yanked away.

Leon coughs and turns to address Teo. "I assume that today's events will remain secret to all those who are not currently in this room?"

"Mia's safety will be our collective priority until a child is born. You have my word no one here will endanger her by revealing your union."

My father relaxes a bit at this news, though he narrows his eyes at the priest, who looks as if he were trying to melt into the background.

Leon nods once before dragging his eyes back to me, suddenly looking unsure. "Then we should depart."

"Right," I manage to whisper.

Cas hugs me again, as does my father. I don't spare a look at Rocco and Teo. Both of them have the common sense to remain silent as I follow Leon out of the room.

There's a numbness that threatens to take hold of me as he guides us to an elevator. I cling to it like a lifeline instead of thinking about what is about to happen.

But there's a stubborn, angry fire that prevents me from succumbing entirely. It's a fire I unleash the second the elevator door closes and we begin our ascent to the highest floor.

"Was it you?" I ask as firmly as I can.

Leon glances down at me with an unreadable expression. "You're shaking. Mia, I'm not going to force you to—"

"Was. It. You."

He sighs. "You're going to have to be a bit more specific."

"Did you or did you not threaten my father's life?"

Something seems to click behind those unfairly gorgeous brown eyes. "That's why you agreed to this?"

"You didn't know?" I frown as a tightness begins to settle within me.

"No, I—" he swallows and looks away. "I need an heir. But there are other…means of acquiring one. I wouldn't need to threaten your father to do so."

I look away, too. There's so much tension in this small

space it's impossible to discern if he's lying or not. Nor do I know him well enough to make a guess from his body language.

"I'm supposed to take you at your word?"

"It makes little difference whether or not you believe me."

The elevator doors slide open, and the relief is instantaneous. Leon steps out promptly, and I follow him into what appears to be the penthouse suit. It's a gorgeous open-plan space with a window that showcases jaw-dropping views of Manhattan.

Well, at least I married into money.

"Would you like a drink?" Leon calls as he wanders over to the kitchen. It seems someone has taken the liberty of stocking our fridge with champagne.

I make my way over to the window for a better look. "Is there anything stronger?"

He doesn't reply, but a few minutes later, he's at my side, handing me a generous glass of whiskey.

I down it in one swallow.

He gives me a long look over the rim of his own glass before placing it down. "We don't have to do this."

"Except we do for the marriage to be viable," I counter.

"No one needs to know."

It was a good point. A strong point, actually. One I wish I'd thought of.

"Unless you'd secretly like to."

My eyes snap away from the skyline to find a dirty little smile on his face. It's the first smile I think I've seen him wear.

I'm instantly on the defensive. "I think there are possibly a million things I'd rather do."

"Am I really so abhorrent to you?" he teases, handing me the rest of his drink to finish.

I see what he's doing; he's trying to make me relax. It's a gesture that I might have considered sweet if we weren't discussing the possibility of sleeping together when we barely know one another.

"You have...agreeable features," I concede as I down the rest of his whiskey, too.

"I've been told they're more than agreeable."

"By who, your mirror?"

Leon chuckles at that. It's a dark sound, one that does things to my stomach, and I find my heart racing again without my permission.

He steps forward slowly, crowding into my space, and for a moment, I think my heart stops entirely.

But then he merely plucks the glass from my hand and pulls away. I do my best to ignore the way his fingers brush against mine, leaving a trail of heat across my skin.

"You're fairly agreeable to look at yourself," he admits as casually as if he were commenting on the weather.

It's infuriating. "You should see me without the dress on."

That does it. That gets me the reaction I was craving. The flash of warmth in his eyes I noticed earlier appears again as his head snaps to me.

And then...

I'm suddenly pressed up against the window. The distance between us decreases to a hair's breadth as his broad chest entirely surrounds me. Rum spice and black pepper and that dirty little smile.

"Would you like that?" His voice is low and thick. Teasing yet sure.

I try to focus, try to think as my senses become overwhelmed by him. "For...consummation purposes," I manage to breathe out, proud of myself for coming up with such a logical excuse under such pressure.

He hums thoughtfully as his head dips down to my ear. "Don't worry, I'll make it good for you."

"You're quite sure of yourself," I say breathlessly, noticing the dark desire in his eyes.

His hand suddenly reaches out, snatching at my thigh, and he hoists it to his hip so that he can slip his leg between mine, pulling our bodies so close there's barely a place we aren't touching.

"I have every reason to be."

I gasp and it's suddenly a game. His eyes are clearly transfixed by my lips, and I want to put them all over his skin. But I can't move first, can't be the first to concede.

"Then get me out of this fucking dress."

It's unnerving in the best way how quickly he manhandles me, spinning me in an instant and pressing my front into the cool glass hard enough for another gasp to escape my lips. His hands make quick of the dress, and I shiver as it falls to the floor.

He releases me, stepping back as I turn to face him.

His expression is positively primal as he takes me in. "You were right."

I quirk an eyebrow and step forward with more confidence than I feel. "About what?"

"This is far more agreeable."

I know the game is going to end the second he reaches for me. And I let it, surrendering to the moment in front of me.

Hands tangle in my hair as he pulls it from my face,

anchoring me there as he dips his head. There's nothing chaste or respectable about this kiss. It's filled with pure, unrestrained desire.

And I hate how easy it is to lose myself to the sensation.

His lips move against mine in perfect tandem with my own, as if we already know this particular dance, as if my body instinctively knows his.

Which is entirely impossible, except it's absolutely insane at the same time.

"Fuck," he breaths across my lips, pulling me impossibly closer, and yet not close enough at all.

His hands are like shackles, firm and large, skimming over every part of my body, holding my neck, my arms, my waist. He finally grips my ass so firmly that I have to stifle a groan.

All the while, his tongue explores mine with that same strange familiarity. I'm locked in battle, desperate to taste and taste and taste.

I bite down on his bottom lip, and suddenly, his hands drop down to my thighs, and I'm being hoisted up.

I'm a little proud that I don't shriek at the sudden loss of balance. I do, however, moan as I wrap my legs around his waist and feel just how hard he is beneath me.

The sound makes him kiss me harder, and his hands grip my thighs even more firmly. It's decisively a very, very possessive gesture and one that makes my heart flutter along with the lust already aching between my legs.

Luckily, Leon seems in no mood to delay our combined relief, walking us back over to the—quite frankly, enormous—bed.

He deposits me on the sheets, and then, with a groan of

annoyance that could have been his or mine for all I can tell at this point, he steps back.

"Look at you," he growls to himself as his eyes bore into my nearly-naked body sprawled before him. The dress hadn't required a bra, but my thong was still traitorously covering my most intimate self.

I watch as Leon makes quick work of his shirt buttons, still staring at me with an intensity that makes my insides squirm.

There's too much heat in that look, too much of *everything*. There's no way I can survive just lying here without any kind of relief.

My hand reaches down between my thighs and pushes my thong to one side.

"What the fuck are you doing?" His voice comes out half-choked, and it's suddenly hard to see where the chocolate of his irises ends and his pupils begin.

I ignore him, letting my fingers relieve some of the tension of watching him undress before me. The slickness of my own pussy makes another moan slip from my lips.

The second I close my eyes to enjoy the sensation, my hand is ripped away from my skin—so hard my thong stings the back of my hand as it snaps completely.

I open my eyes (and mouth) to complain, only to find Leon looming over me, his arm pinning my hand above my head. He is deliciously naked.

"I said I'd make it good for you," he says, shifting upward to allow his own hand to take up residence where mine had been a moment before. In doing so, he gives me an eyeful of his hardened cock for the first time.

I'm not sure if I gasp at his touch between his legs or at the sheer *size* of his package.

Either way, I arch my back, close my eyes, and try to squish down the fear that prickles across my skin. There's no possible way I'd be able to take him. I've never even *seen* a man that big, and he dwarfs my usual toys by a significant margin.

He might actually break me in two.

But all conscious thought and worry is brutally interrupted by the presence of his tongue on my clit.

I'd barely noticed him drifting downward, so distracted by internal panic about the size of his cock, but now every fiber of my being feels like it's been lit on fire.

"Holy shit, holy shit, holy shit," a voice that sounds like a strangled version of mine begins to chant.

I clench around the finger he has already inside me, then groan as another joins it, opening me up wider and wider. I'm now slick with a seemingly unending amount of wetness.

He hums his approval against the most sensitive point of me, and my fingers find themselves pulling desperately at his hair. If he doesn't stop soon…

The third finger pushes me over that edge. Agonizingly slow and deep, I feel the exact moment his knuckles enter me, and a cry is ripped violently from my vocal cords.

I slam my pelvis into his hand as hard as I can, riding out my orgasm without inhibition, too lost in the feeling of pleasure to think about the situation or the ridiculous hugeness of his throbbing cock hovering threateningly nearby.

Absently, I'm aware that I'm not being quiet. Sounds tumble out of my mouth until I slowly begin to come back to some awareness, and the release fizzles out into glorious satisfaction.

I feel completely and utterly spent.

Which makes my poor, frazzled brain quite confused when Leon's face appears above me and a firmness presses against my core where his tongue and fingers had just been.

"Consummation," he informs the probably vacant look on my face.

Vaguely, I know the word is important. Vaguely, I'm aware I might have had reservations about this. But I can't think of anything more crucial than giving my absolute consent to this man to do whatever the fuck he wants with me.

The pressure between my legs slowly begins to increase, and I open myself wide to accommodate him. I am thoroughly distracted by the kisses now being planted across my chest and up my neck.

Leon's hand reaches down to coat his length in my juices, but he kisses me at the same time, and all I can focus on is the taste of myself in his mouth.

He fills me inch my glorious inch, slowly and carefully. I begin to get impatient. That ache is already building up again, and I am desperate for some kind of friction.

Without warning, I buck my hips up to meet him.

"FUCK!" I scream as he's suddenly driven so deep within me that I see stars.

His hands immediately clamp down on my waist, pulling me away. "Don't do that."

"What the FUCK!"

"We need to go slowly," he insists as he pushes into me again with deliberate care.

This time, I'm more prepared, and with a new sense of clarity, I allow him to take back control. He's carefully working me open, as he has been doing this whole time, I realize with a start.

My body instantly begins to relax as it warms to the sensation of his huge length inside me. I find myself whimpering every time he withdraws.

"Are you all right?" his concerned voice whispers in my ear.

"Just fucking fuck me."

He needs no more encouragement than that, and I begin to moan again as that aching pressure builds within me once more at the friction of his increasingly hurried strokes.

Time seems to stop and start and stretch and then suddenly, his mouth catches one of my moans as he presses his lips down hard against my own.

The kiss causes pleasure to sing through me just as Leon picks up the pace once more, and I feel myself nearing the edge again.

This time, when I fall off, Leon comes with me.

He clings to me as he spills within me, hands digging into me hard enough to bruise, but I can't bring myself to care. I want this feeling to last and last and last.

Sex doesn't feel like this. It's never felt like this.

And yet, as I sit in the aftermath of my ecstasy, I can't help but be confronted with an absolute truth: sex with Leon was more incredible than anything else I had ever experienced in my life.

4
LEON

My eyes snap open the second I feel the bed jostle beneath me the next morning.

I find Mia halfway off the bed—clearly making an attempt at escape—and staring at me like a deer in headlights.

"Good morning," I say pleasantly.

She returns the greeting under her breath as she stands and makes her way over to the closet.

In the morning light, it's very hard not to stare at her naked form. The perfectly smooth, slightly bronzed skin of her back. The tight roundness of her ass that is already sporting purplish bruises from the night before.

My mind drifts back of its own accord. The way she'd sounded, the way she had moved against me, all of it had been unnervingly divine. The thought alone was already making me hard again.

I shake my head, reminding myself quite forcefully that casual sex was never part of this arrangement. Mia only agreed to this in order to fulfill her duties to the Guild...and to satisfy whomever threatened her father.

With no small effort, I glue my eyes to Mia's face, vowing not to look any lower than her neck.

When she opens the closet doors, she seems genuinely surprised by the large selection of clothes within.

"Are you living here?" she asks as she helps herself to a pair of shorts and a T-shirt that will likely drown her.

"Temporarily," I reply. "I've recently purchased a more... ah...family-appropriate property just off Central Park West."

If I hadn't been staring at her face, I might have missed the split second that she looked impressed. "A brownstone?"

I make an affirmative noise. "It will be ready in a few days."

With a small stretch, I reach over to grab a bathrobe and make a beeline for the kitchen. Coffee was certainly in order.

I'm about halfway through brewing it, when there's a patter of feet behind me.

"Do you expect me to live with you?" she asks carefully.

I consider this for a moment. Part of the deal was that I do everything in my power to ensure her safety, which would be considerably easier if I had eyes on her at all times.

But then again, I doubt such a suggestion would go down well. Considering we seem to have reached a temporary truce, I'm not in the mood to be on the receiving end of her yelling again.

"Eventually, but there's no pressing need until the baby is born," I say.

"Right," her voice sounds distant, distracted, and when I turn to hand her a coffee, her face matches the tone of her voice. She glances down at the offering. "I don't drink coffee."

"Noted."

There's an awkward pause as I put the cup down. I rack my brain for something to ask her, to put her at ease again.

She looks so lovely wearing my clothes, I realize with a start. Her red curls are the right kind of messy to be considered charming and warmth just seems to radiate from her so naturally.

It wouldn't be a bad thing to make the most of this situation. Perhaps we could even be friends.

I'm about to say as much when she breaks the silence for me.

"I suppose we don't really need to know each other, do we?"

Her words turn my own to ash in my mouth. Right. Duty. None of this is personal.

"No. We don't." I drain the rest of my coffee, though it tastes much more bitter now, and deposit the mug in the sink with a little too much force. The handle breaks off with a small crack.

I ignore it as I storm past her back into the bedroom, quickly finding clothes of my own before gathering my necessities for the day. Suddenly, spending the morning alone with her feels absolutely abhorrent.

"What...what do I do now?" her voice asks quietly from the corner.

I pocket my phone and glance in the mirror. Respectable, professional. Cold. "Stay as long as you want, but I have to go. I'll send my new address to Teo if you need it."

"Wouldn't it be easier to exchange numbers?"

"Do what you want."

"But what about—"

I turn on her, suddenly very irritated indeed by her incessant nagging. "I don't care, all right? I'm not your keeper, and, quite frankly, I have more important things to worry about than this. You stick to upholding your part of the agreement, and I'll stick to mine. Agreed?"

Mia looks somewhat overwhelmed by my outburst, and so frightfully vulnerable in those oversized clothes. I have to look away so that she doesn't see the guilt in my gaze.

This is decidedly the wrong thing to do, as her voice suddenly takes a harder edge.

"Oh, of course, my dear husband. Let me bend over backward to fulfill my wifely duties. How would you like me next time? Spread eagle or with a bag over my fucking head?"

I refuse to dignify her response with even a glance as I pack up my things. The cold shoulder does nothing to improve Mia's mood, and she promptly leaves the room.

A second later, the door to the penthouse slams shut behind her.

IT TAKES the entirety of the drive to the Prince's Hand's flagship casino for me to shake the bitterness that threatens to choke me.

I always knew this marital arrangement would be a strain at best, but it was foolish of me to think it could be anything more. Getting my hopes up was nothing short of embarrassing.

As I step across the familiar entranceway, I let the

embarrassment fall at my feet, cloaking myself in the things that truly matter. The most important of which is survival for the sake of my sister.

By the time I made it to the meeting room, the morning's interaction with my unwilling wife was tightly locked away at the very back of my mind.

"Natali," Dante greets me with an easy smirk, though I note he looks particularly gleeful today.

He's one of the first to arrive, as has become his habit since the Guild saw fit to send one of their own men to help negotiate an alliance. Teo's second was, admittedly, a point of tension to begin with.

But over the last few months, I've found that he's grown on me some. Dante's easy-going nature and extensive understanding of trade routes with our counterparts across the globe have been invaluable.

"Is it your birthday or something?" I give him a once-over—yes, his knee is bouncing beneath the table.

Dante taps the folder before him. "An early birthday present, perhaps."

I quirk an eyebrow at him. If what he's implying is true... damn it, the Guild works fast.

I take a seat at the end of the table and wait for the rest of the men to filter in. Most greet me with a tight nod as they enter.

Many of my men are from the old guard, left over from when my father and mother were running the Prince's Hand, too set in their ways now to break away from me despite the looming alliance with a rival mafioso.

Most have now, thankfully, conceded on the merits of said alliance, but it's still a relief when Maximilian shows up. The younger man throws me a half-hearted salute as he sits at the other end of the table.

He's fresh blood courtesy of my relationship with the Californians. Max has added a sense of...relevance to the upper rankings of the Prince's Hand that has been sorely missing. His competency has been an added bonus these last few months.

Once everyone finally settles in, Dante is practically bouncing in his seat.

I sigh and hold him off with a gesture of my hand. "Before we begin, I want a report on the Cartel bombings."

It's been a growing concern these last few weeks. Small bombs had been placed near the homes of various known lieutenants, and from Teo's reports, they were targeting the Guild, too.

That threat is one of the other reasons I'd decided to relocate.

Max clears his throat to address the room. "Lab results are back. It was hydrogen, as we expected. But whoever is making them for the Cartel is barely giving them enough kick to take down a car, let alone a building."

"Would it be possible if they planted multiple of the deVitales?"

"Possibly, but it would be incredibly inefficient. Why place ten small bombs when you could plant one big one? But nothing about the pattern of attacks suggests they're even entertaining the idea of anything bigger."

Dante considers this a moment. "So this is a scare tactic."

"Or they have a limited supply of materials," Max offers. "We know the Cartel doesn't have the same relationship with local authorities that we do. Trying to secure destructive materials could prove more difficult for them without raising legal suspicion."

Something about the way Max phrased that made my mind jump five theories ahead. "Unless they're trying to provoke us to retaliate in kind. I imagine it's easier to steal materials that have already been stolen from someone else."

Max immediately nods in understanding. He was good like that.

"Sorry, what?" Dante looks at me in confusion.

Max does the courtesy of explaining. "It would be far easier for us to create explosives without the authorities getting involved. They may well be waiting for us to do so. That way, they can just target our labs to supply themselves without the hassle."

"Keep monitoring the bombs, Max. Dante, report our suspicions to Teo. I want to know if he has a secure facility we could repurpose as a lab."

Dante smirks. "You seem very sure he'll be receptive to your demands."

The entire table looks at him curiously.

I roll my eyes and gesture for him to take the floor. "All right, tell us the news."

Dante stands and drops a folder before me dramatically. "You might be interested in reading that."

It's quite anti-climatic considering how thin the legal document inside the folder is. Though I suppose *legal* isn't the term one would necessarily associate with it.

"For the rest of the room," I monotone as I read through the contract, "our esteemed representative of the Guild has just handed me a contract of alliance."

A murmur quickly spreads among my peers as I continue to read and get to the bottom of the page. My eyebrows dart up in surprise at what I find at the bottom of the document.

"It appears that Teo Vitale and his second, Dante Grasso, have already signed it." I look at the latter in surprise. "I thought Teo would at least want to play chicken about who signed first."

Dante smirks. "I think we're all excited to get this over with."

Now that I've met the Guild's terms, I suppose there isn't much point in waiting around.

I glance out at the expectant faces of those at my table, some even standing to get a better view of the document. My fingers inch toward my pen.

"I guess there's no point in delaying," I murmur as I go to sign—only to freeze when I notice the box next to mine and under Dante's signature.

I still need a second.

There wasn't a concrete reason as to why I had put off appointing someone new. Perhaps because the position had been filled by my sister for so long, it was difficult to imagine anyone else at my side.

But as I look around the room at the faces that have watched me grow from boy to man, there are frighteningly few options that could possibly fill Isabella's stiletto-wearing, computer-hacking, no-shit-taking place.

Oddly, Mia suddenly springs to mind. I bury the thought quickly.

"Maximilian," I call out absently. "Come here a moment."

There's the sound of a chair being dragged across the floor, followed by his footsteps. Everyone else seems to be collectively holding their breath.

I don't speak again until he's at my shoulder. "Would you be so kind as to sign here for me?" I point to the space in question.

Max does not move. "Is this your way of asking me to be your second?"

"Would you prefer a ring?" I wince as soon as the words leave my mouth. Too soon.

But Max doesn't seem to notice. He smirks as he plucks the pen from my hand and scrawls his name in a surprisingly elegant script.

Once I've done the same, I risk looking up at our audience.

Dante, at least, seems pleased with this development. The rest seem torn between relief that the negotiations are finally over and staring daggers at Max.

It's to be expected, considering he's a newcomer, but luckily, Max doesn't seem too concerned by their judgment.

"There we have it," I announce as I hand the contract back to Dante. "Tell Teo I am looking forward to a very happy matrimony."

5

MIA

"Teo Vitale, OPEN THIS FUCKING DOOR!" I yell because if I don't yell, I might cry, and being angry right now is a lot damn easier than being sad.

It took me a long time to track him down. Longer than it should have, which is enough to tell me that he's trying to hide. Especially as he seems to have locked himself up in the one place he presumed I'd never look.

The *Candelabra* was always empty this time of day, save for the cleaning crew resetting everything for the evening crowd. It's always a bit strange seeing the stage drenched in sunlight.

The Guild's office is usually only used as a private space to entertain honored guests during the show. But Teo has been known to work from it whenever the Guild's base—a large industrial unit by the docks—gets too crowded.

A fact I assume he must have thought I'd forgotten.

"YOU CAN'T HIDE IN THERE FOREVER!"

I can hear someone shuffling behind it and wait another moment before pounding against the wood once more.

"I HAVE A MASTER KEY, YOU KNOW. I WILL MURDER YOU IF I HAVE TO GO GET IT."

I don't have a master key, but I *am* the manager, so it's not out of the realm of possibilities.

Suddenly, there's a resigned sigh and a click, and the door swings an inch inward.

Teo gives me an exasperated look through the crack. "There is no master key."

I ignore him and push through the door.

"You've been avoiding me," I state as soon as I get far enough inside to spin around and face him.

He mutters something suspiciously, like, "Can you blame me?" and then closes the door again. He takes heavy steps back toward the desk, where he seems to have been poring over several documents.

Teo picks up a thin file and hands it to me. "Here. You may as well see what you accomplished."

Curiosity momentarily overriding my anger, I take the file and examine it. I stare at the name signed at the bottom for a beat too long. "It's happened, then?"

"For the first time in recorded history, the Italian mafioso of Brooklyn and Manhattan have committed to an alliance. If people knew of the importance of such things, they'd probably hang that," he gestures to the file, "in a museum."

I snap the file closed and place it back on the desk. "You must be proud of your legacy," I say sarcastically.

"*Your* legacy. None of this would have happened if it weren't for your..."

I save him the trouble of finding the word. "Sacrifice?"

"I was going to say *commitment*."

"That's funny because the last time you asked me to commit to the Guild, it didn't involve blackmailing me with my father's life."

Teo does a double-take at me. "I *what*?"

I've known Teo Vitale for a long time. Too long, really. The genuine surprise on his face causes my anger to cool briefly.

"I'm only going to ask you this once." I hope the seriousness of my tone infers that I expect an earnest answer. "Did you or did you not threaten my father's life if I did not go ahead with the marriage?"

Teo does not drop my gaze for even a second. "I did not. I would have never."

There's a moment of silence as I assess his words, his intonation, his most minor facial expressions.

Leon Natali may have claimed he hadn't threatened my father's life. But I don't know him like I know Teo. And there is nothing about Teo Vitale that indicates that he's lying to me right now.

The realization hits me a second later.

Leon had lied.

He'd lied, and then I'd slept with him.

The dam my anger had built against the onslaught of my misery began to crack. I blink away the tears in my eyes.

"Right," I say, deflating away from discussion of the don. Suddenly, I'm very aware that I had threatened his life only a few moments ago.

Teo is watching me infuriatingly closely. "Did he threaten you?" His voice is cold, measured. Calculating.

I shake my head. "It was just something my father said."

He swiftly picks up the thin file again and pushes it between us. "I will rip this contract in two—"

I snatch it from him. "Don't be so fucking dramatic. You said it yourself: this is a momentous occasion."

Teo only stares at me, unwilling to back down until I give him something more.

"It's worth it, isn't it?" I remind him. "This fight against the Cartel, Amos Rubio...you need the Prince's Hand. It's me marrying him, or it's the lives of everyone else. I'm not comfortable having their blood on my hands."

Slowly, his gaze softens. "I didn't want to ask this of you."

"But the Guild was already asking you to do something about me, right? It makes sense," I allow. "I hate it, but it makes sense. Your hands were tied."

He runs said hand through his hair in exasperation. "Speaking of..."

I sit down heavily in one of the armchairs, already bracing myself for the worst. "Oh God, what?"

"You're not a part of the Guild anymore. Not that you were before, but now that you're on the more...Manhattan side of things, we think it's best you step down from your position here."

"You mean..."

"I will write your recommendation personally. Anywhere you want to go, I'll put a word in."

Something horrendously numb threatens to swallow my entire body. I've worked at the *Candelabra* since I was old enough to serve a drink. Now, even that was being taken from me.

"Right."

"Word of adVitale? Stick to something managerial. The Guild barely tolerated your more mercantile activities, even with your father always there to defend you. I doubt the Prince's Hand will take so well to it."

Through the fog of numbness, a single dreadful thought pushes to the forefront. "How am I supposed to afford rent?"

Teo gives me an odd look.

I suppose it would have never really occurred to him that I would ever *need* my job in that way. My father remains Teo's master of finance and loans, supplementing Guild activities with the generosity of his own vast estate.

But living on the blood money of a mafioso was never something I wanted. Working as a server, a bartender, and a manager was my sole source of income. It was enough to keep me afloat, to lead an honest life.

Well...

Except for those moments when that wasn't exactly true.

Dire moments when my father asked me to collect on a loan. Or there was a particularly interesting job listed on the dark web that required someone with my particular skill set.

That was where the money I had used to get myself through college had come from. I promised myself that after I graduated, I would stop.

And I had, for the most part.

Only now...

Teo interrupts my thoughts with a confused sort of expression. "You understand that Leon Natali is your husband, right? Even if you didn't want to live with him, he's a billionaire, Mia. *You* are a billionaire now."

Like that's any better than accepting blood money from my father. But it's not a discussion I felt like having right now when I could feel the dam crumbling more and more by the second.

I changed the topic entirely, suddenly very eager to leave before I fell apart. "Leon said he'd send you his new address."

To his credit, Teo doesn't ask why he didn't send it to me himself as he swipes up his phone to forward it to me.

I nod as my cell pings with the notification and turn to leave. "Sorry for threatening to kill you," I murmur over my shoulder.

Teo begins to say something, then stops himself. Then pushes through anyway. "I'm sorry that it was you. I hope...I hope you can find something good in all of this."

I can't reply for fear of the sob that threatens to burst from my chest.

I'm not entirely sure how I got here. One second, I was getting into my car, the next, I was getting out of it.

The front door is unfamiliar but overwhelmingly grand as I stand before it. I feel so ridiculously fragile that even the act of knocking feels like it could be enough to tip me over into my misery.

I hear footsteps and use whatever is left of my resilience to brace myself for what comes next.

The door opens, and...

"Mia?"

Cassandra's eyes are wide with concern, matching, with almost scary similarity, the infant balancing on her hip.

I swallow hard. "Can I—"

I'm cut off by my friend slamming into me, her free arm pulling me in close.

The dam breaks.

The sobs tear through my body like a freight train, unrelenting in their brutality. There are more than a few moments that I think I might completely collapse if it wasn't for Cas propping me up.

"It's okay, it's okay," she says soothingly as she rubs my back. "Come on, come inside. That's it."

I let her lead me in, somewhat dizzy from the effort of dispelling a horrendous amount of water from my eyes. If I wasn't so exhausted, I might have felt slightly embarrassed.

But Cas remains, first and foremost, my best friend, and perhaps the only person on the planet that I feel comfortable enough to be comforted by.

"Denise!" Cas calls out, and the stern British woman seems to materialize out of thin air. "Will you take Cory back to his room?"

The sweet-faced baby makes grabby hands at his mother as Denise extracts him, and Cas leads me to a couch.

I can't look her in the eye as she sits next to me, mainly because I'm still crying, but also because I know as soon as I look at her again, her sympathy will only make it worse.

"I'll get you some water," she says after a moment, going to stand. "Or do we need something stronger?"

"Water is f-fine," I manage to choke out.

She says nothing more as she leaves me there on her far too comfortable couch. Alone in her new living room, I find myself picking up my legs and lying down properly—covering myself with a blanket.

Never have I ever felt sorrier for myself. Everything that's happened these last few days batters me over and over again.

The Guild catching up to me. The threat against my father's life. Agreeing to marry Leon Natali. Agreeing to have his children. The lying, then sleeping with him. How good it felt in the moment and how awful it felt in the morning.

I can't help but look back and try to come up with a scenario where none of this happened.

If I had been more subtle with my mercenary work...if I'd stepped away from this life when I had the chance, none of this would have happened.

At some point, Cas returns with both water and whiskey and sits on the end of the couch, lifting my head up to rest it on her knee.

Her fingers softly stroke through my hair as the tears continue to flow and flow and flow.

"I'm sorry," she whispers over and over.

"It's not your fault," I manage eventually. "It's my fault."

Her fingers stop their soothing motions. "Well, that's absolutely not true."

"It is, though. If I'd just agreed to join the Guild before all of this, I would never have been forced to marry that lying asshole. I can't even think about being in the same room as him again, let alone..." my breathing catches, and I cry again.

"If you want to blame anyone for this, blame Teo," Cas counters. "Better yet, blame Amos Rubio for forcing the alliance in the first place."

I sniff into her lap, and the hair stroking resumes.

"I know you don't like him." There's no need for me to ask who she's talking about. "But I don't think he's so bad, really. You remember he saved my life once? His sister speaks quite highly of him, too. Plus, he's not the worst-looking guy in the world."

I groan a little. "You're seriously comforting me by saying, 'at least the guy you're forced to sleep with is hot'?"

"Silver linings?"

"He threatened my father's life, Cas," I explain bitterly. "He can parade about his glowing reputation to everyone else, but he lied to my face so that we would consummate our marriage."

This is news to Cassandra, who immediately sits me up and demands the full story. So, I tell her. I tell her about my father's words, the night in the penthouse, and my conversation with Teo. By the time I'm finished, Cas looks absolutely furious.

"I could kill him," she seethes. "I *will* kill him."

"He's integral to the alliance," I point out, suddenly feeling utterly exhausted.

"I'm going to think about killing him really, really hard."

This makes me laugh for the first time in what feels like days.

Cas watches me with a new kind of determination in her eyes. "You need to take back control."

I lean back on the couch. "How the hell am I supposed to do that? This is already so out of my control. I'm already drowning."

"He might have won the first match, Mia, but this is a long game, and you still have a chance to win the upper hand. You still have me and Rocco and Teo on your side."

"I don't know if I can do it," I whisper. I thought I was out of tears, but one drips down my cheek anyway.

"You can," she leans in to wrap her arms around me. "You're going to be a *mother*. You *will* be a mother on your own terms, and he will not take that from you. Do you hear me?"

I feel something in me break a bit at her words. "What kind of mother lets something like this happen?"

"You, Maddison, will be an incredible mother. How many times have you been there for me? Hell, you walked into that wedding willing to put everything on the line for your father. Your child will be so, so lucky to have you. So fight for them."

Not for me, not for Leon. For my child.

"Okay."

"Okay?"

"Let's take back control."

6

LEON

The celebrations of signing the alliance all too quickly fell away to the actual work involved with said alliance.

I'm not entirely sure when the light began to fade and the moon began to rise. I only stopped to switch on my desk light once the documents on my desk became too difficult to read.

At one point, the casino's manager—Simon—had arrived with dinner and coffee. It was a habit he'd picked up after years of my sister chastising me for staying on top of meals when I was working late.

There was a stack of emails in my inbox pertaining to the merging of forces, borrowing of specialists, and access to resources. Sharing and caring from one mafioso to another.

However, the documents I was currently perusing were all intel-oriented. They were slowly allowing me to piece together a full picture of the Cartel's influence over the last few years.

Amos Rubio was a drug kingpin who operated in Brooklyn. Interaction with the Prince's Hand's Manhattan casinos had been limited until recently.

Until my sister married Teo Vitale, and suddenly, the Guild seemed like a much more considerable threat. Until I'd burned down a building in Brooklyn, and the Cartel had taken that personally.

The intel in my hand currently was particularly engrossing, detailing how Giuliano Moretti had framed a man for being a mole in the Guild, only to be discovered supplying information directly to Amos Rubio himself...

"Hey!"

I almost drop the pages as I jump at the sound. My attention immediately snaps to the stern-looking blonde before me.

"Isabella," I greet her as casually as I can, putting everything back on the desk with all the ease of a man who was absolutely not caught off guard.

The quirk of her eyebrow tells me she doesn't believe it for a second. "I cleared my throat like four times."

"I'm busy," I say instead of responding to that. "Did you need something?"

"An invite to my brother's wedding would have been nice. But I suppose it's a bit late for that."

Ah. Right.

She crosses her arms and gives me a long, hard stare—so reminiscent of how our mother used to look at me that I almost flinch back in my chair.

"Teo wanted it to be an intimate affair," I reply, unashamedly throwing the man under the bus. "No one was supposed to know."

"I'm your *sister*."

"Take it up with your husband."

A fist slams down on my desk. I don't flinch. "I don't care what Teo did or did not want. I wanted *you* to want me there."

I meet her eyes—the same brown as mine, though somehow hers always seem so much deeper. "Had it been a wedding and not a business transaction, I would have made you my best man. That better?"

"A business transaction with *vows*, Leon. In front of a priest." She throws her hands up in exasperation. "She has your last name now, for fuck's sake."

"You didn't miss anything important." I try not to sound bitter. I try not to think about anything that would make me feel bitter. Or anyone. "You knew it was a possibility, and it all happened quite quickly in the end."

Isabella's eyes squint slightly. "I never thought you'd actually go through with it."

"What choice did I have?"

"If this is about heirs—"

"Of course, it's about heirs!" I feel my voice rising and try to reign it in. "You've married into the Guild. Mother is dead. There's no one left here but me, and I can't protect the people I love forever."

Her expression softens. "That's not your responsibility."

"I'm your brother. You and Irina are the only family I have left. Of course, it's my responsibility, Issy."

Isabella's shoulders sag as she flops down into the chair opposite me. "I can't believe Irina will have to call her Aunty Mia now."

I grunt noncommittally. I hadn't even thought about introducing my wife to what was left of my family.

"You know, the first time I met her, she screamed in my

face for disrupting Cas and Rocco's wedding and put a knife to my throat?" Isabella grimaces as she says it.

I grimace back. "The first time I met her, she nearly choked me to death with her thighs."

Isabella's mouth twitches up at the unspoken innuendo.

"Don't," I point at her before she can start. "It wasn't exactly a happy reunion."

"I can't imagine why she'd even agree to marry you, honestly."

I shrug. "She seemed to be under the impression that her father's life was at stake if she didn't."

Isabella blinks at me. "Who the hell threatened Marco?"

"No idea. She thought it was me. I thought it must have been Teo."

"Teo wouldn't," she says with a firm belief in her husband, which I'm glad at least one of us holds.

"Either way, it happened. We're married, it's...it's legal." I quickly skirt over exactly *how* legal it all is. "Mia Chiavari is a Natali now. That's all you really missed."

Isabella sighs and looks away from my desk, suddenly looking quite tired. "Can you give me a real reason?"

"I told you, I need an heir. The alliance needs me to have an heir, and I need the alliance to keep you safe."

"Oh, screw the damn alliance for a second, all right?" she brushes me off entirely. "Why are *you* doing this?"

For a moment, I contemplate not telling her at all. My reasoning had been enough to satisfy both Teo and Mia before. They hadn't needed anything else.

But I also know that Isabella wasn't going to drop this. She needed to know that I had something at stake here beyond duty.

"I...a child, Issy. A fresh start for the Natali name. One that's not tainted by...by *her*," I admit finally.

Memories of my mother are always jarring to remember. The softness with which she nurtured Issy, the harshness of her disapproval of me. Until, one day, she'd turned that harshness on Issy.

The day she'd threatened her life.

I knew then the crone that I'd only tentatively called my mother had shown that she was a monster all along. Her love for Issy had been her only redeeming factor.

I sleep peacefully, knowing her blood is on my hands.

The same hands Isabella now reaches for, squeezing them gently in her own. "You already carry the Natali name so beautifully, brother."

"Now there's two of us," I reply, though my voice lacks the emotion to make it sound lighthearted.

This makes her eyes narrow again. "Is it...do you think that maybe you two could, you know..."

"No," I say firmly. "Like I said. It was a business transaction. She has no interest in me beyond holding up her side of the agreement."

Isabella gives me a speculative look. One that sees far too much and makes me stand up from my desk. It's getting late anyway, and I'm not sure how much I want to continue this conversation.

Thankfully, she seems to take the cue and stands as well.

"You'll be careful with this, won't you, Leon?" she asks quietly as she watches me pull on my coat.

"Always am."

IT'S strange not to be heading back to the hotel tonight. But Max had taken on overseeing the protection of the brownstone, and the family home had been prepared for me in record time.

Yet another reason to be thankful for the competency of my new second. Not that Max knew that my wife would soon be residing there, but it put me at ease knowing she could be there as soon as she got pregnant.

It was also a far nicer feeling walking up the steps of a family home than the impersonal elevator ride to a penthouse that lacked any personal artifacts.

The key twists in the door, and the warm light in the tall entranceway greets me. Already, a few pictures are hanging on the walls. The Caravaggio I purchased from a black market dealer in Italy hung pride of place.

I take in the familiar contrasts and brushstrokes as I loosen the tie from my neck and discard my jacket.

A drink, I think, *is needed after that conversation with my sister*. It's already late, and I'll likely need to be there early again tomorrow. But right now, I can deal with a little indulgence, so I walk into the kitchen with a purpose.

Working hard on the alliance has made for quite a wonderful distraction. But now, alone in this empty house, there's nothing but the biting loneliness to prevent me from thinking about a certain redhead and the way she sounds when she moans my name.

As soon as that floodgate opens, it's very, very hard to stop it.

It's too easy to remember her little gasp as I entered her, to imagine how she might look bent over the kitchen counter, how her nails might rake over my skin, how she might taste in my mouth.

It's almost too easy to picture her sitting there at the breakfast bar, regarding me with a slow blink, brutally emotionless, knowing exactly what it takes to crack that facade.

I reach up for a glass.

Then, turn back to the breakfast bar.

She's still there.

Very real. And very, really there.

For the second time today, a woman has managed to take advantage of my preoccupation.

"Leon," she greets me with such shortness that it immediately puts me on edge.

I give myself a beat to relax against the counter and take her in. She's dressed in her own clothes this time, not a fancy dress or a haphazardly thrown-together outfit from my wardrobe.

Her sense of style is...agreeable. Tight jeans hug her curves before flaring out over her boots. The color of her black blouse makes her skin seem almost luminous under the kitchen lights, which pick out the red and gold in her hair as it drapes over her shoulder.

"I wasn't expecting you so soon," I say, glad at how even my voice comes out.

She regards me without concern for my very obvious appraisal. "Don't worry. I have no intention of staying any longer than I need to."

Of course. I go back to finding myself a drink and wait for her to get to whatever point she needs to.

Luckily, it doesn't take her long at all.

"I think we need to establish some ground rules."

My hand hovers over the whiskey bottle for a beat. "I assume you mean about our marriage?"

"What else would I be talking about?"

I smirk slightly, "I could think of a couple of things."

When I turn back to her, her mouth is set in a thin line. "Number one. No flirtation."

"We're getting right into it, are we?"

"Number two. No sex unless I'm ovulating."

I overpour my measure of whiskey. I need a bigger glass for the whiskey that this conversation is fast requiring.

"Makes sense," I recover quickly. "Do you have an app or something?"

Finally, something other than indifference colors her expression. "*You* won't be monitoring me."

"So what, I'm just going to have to trust you?"

"Yes," she says firmly enough for me not to push it any further.

"Number three," I say instead. "You will do a pregnancy test every day after your cycle."

"Don't you trust me?"

I don't answer that. I take a sip of my whiskey.

Mia chews the inside of her mouth. "Number four. We stay out of each other's business."

"No."

"No?"

"I'm aware that you have sometimes undertaken...freelance work." I give her a hard look. "I want to know if the urge presents itself again so that I can assess the safety implications of said work and the impact it might have on the Prince's Hand."

She scoffs at this. "I think I can assess that for myself, thanks."

"I vowed to keep you safe."

"I didn't marry a babysitter."

"No, you married a don," I say firmly, taking a step forward. "You will respect my wishes, especially those concerning your well-being."

She remains at the breakfast bar, but her glare is hot enough to burn through my skull.

"The thing about respect, Leon, is that you have to earn it." She tilts her head to one side. "And you've done nothing but lie to me since you put this ring on my finger."

7
MIA

I watch Leon carefully as my words register.

For a moment, there's a ghost of something reminiscent of regret that flashes behind his eyes. But he quickly schools his expression into something more neutral as he takes another sip of his drink.

"I'll save us an argument, shall I?" he says once he puts his glass back down.

His lips are damp with whiskey. I don't stare. I don't.

"I deny whatever you're accusing me of. You don't believe me because I've not given you any reason to. Which leads to another fruitless discussion regarding the likelihood of ever being able to trust each other and one of us storming out the room."

"I don't storm," I say petulantly.

Leon regards me for a thoughtful moment. "No, you're correct. You *scorch*."

The way he says it sounds more like a compliment, which only serves to rile me up more.

"Seeing as you have us both all figured out, I suppose there's nothing left for us to say." I step off the stool and stand before him, suddenly quite close to him. "If you will excuse me, I apparently have some earth to scorch."

For a moment, he doesn't move an inch. He looks down at me intensely, and I try not to feel crowded by him, try not to remember how it felt to be held in his embrace. I try not to think of his lips on my neck.

We were closer than this then. We could be close again.

His eyes drop lower.

We could...I could...

I push into him roughly, and the surprise of the movement makes him stumble back a step. It gives me the opening I need to leave, and I take it.

I don't anticipate the speed of his recovery.

Hands grab the wrists that pushed him, pinning them down to the counter behind me.

He's suddenly much, much closer. His chest presses firmly into mine as he holds me right there, entirely at his disposal. Black pepper and rum spice overwhelm my senses.

"This doesn't have to be difficult." His breath is in my ear, my neck. My hands would shake if they weren't pinned down. "I could make this very, very good for you."

He can hear my heartbeat, I'm sure of it. I can feel it trying to burst out of my chest. Betrayed by my body, I feel myself tilting away from him, exposing more of my neck.

"I don't want any of this," I say to try and rectify my actions, but it comes out in a whisper.

Lips press just below my ear. "None of it?"

It takes every morsel of strength I can muster to remind myself why I'm here. Why *we're* here. I struggle to remember who this man is to me beyond the way he can touch me, the way he can bring me to life with only his words.

His touch, his kiss, it's all torture. It's so warm, and it feels so right. I need so much more.

But I can't want more. Not from a man who has manipulated me at every turn. Even now, even this. It's not real.

"I don't want *you*."

He pulls away so sharply it's an effort not to stumble forward. What was once warm and enticing is now ice cold.

Leon turns away, picking up his discarded glass and downing the amber liquid in one swallow. "So be it."

I'm not sure if it's pride or horror that carries my legs toward the exit. Either way, it's a miracle I can move at all.

I came here to regain some control over the situation, not to remind myself how powerless I am as soon as he draws too close. It's agonizing and painful and...

"Mia," his voice calls out after me.

My hand freezes on the door handle. I don't turn around, but I don't open it either.

"You have your own room here. If you ever need it."

For when you eventually move in, he doesn't say.

I push down on the handle and escape into the night without looking back.

"We thought you were dead, you know," Rufin greets me at the back of an Irish bar in New Jersey.

This is an old haunt from a life I swore I'd leave behind after college.

"You have so little faith in me?" I say back, pulling away from the wall to take a measure of the man before me.

I'm not sure if his real name *is* Rufin, but it's what he's always insisted on. He hasn't changed much since I last saw him—same leather jacket, same burn scar across his face. He must be older than me by a decade or so, but I never learned his exact age.

Seeing his face again ignites adrenaline within me that does wonders for my efforts to forget a certain towering blonde man and all the lies that drop from his mouth.

This is what I need, to do something that I can actually control. Something that I'm good at.

"You stopped showing up." He shrugs with a smirk on his half-ruined lips. "I poured a drink out for you and everything."

"Didn't realize you cared."

This used to be my life before the *Candelabra* became my domain. But with that gone, it was either waste away at home, staring at the clock until it was time to perform my wifely duties, or this.

This hasn't changed. Rufin hasn't changed. I don't need to change, either.

He shakes his head. "Something came up last week. I actually thought of you for it, you know. Weird that you would come back now."

I give him a calculating look. "How coincidental."

He seems to weigh his thoughts carefully before responding. "Client seemed a little too keen to know about you. I'd say it's just a coincidence, but keep your guard up anyway."

Rufin digs his hand into his pocket and pulls out a small notebook. From inside, he extracts a business card and offers it to me.

"I always do," I take it from him. There's nothing on it but a number. "Anything I should know?"

"She wanted a woman in her twenties—"

My eyebrow quirks up. "*She*?"

Rufin nods. "Private muscle for a couple of events."

"Babysitting then," I look back down at the card. I can't remember the last time I did freelance work for a woman. Not in this particular industry.

"I'm not sure who she's affiliated with, but it's not the Irish."

I tap the card against my palm a few times. "Thanks, Rufin. I'll send you your cut."

"Can't accept money from a ghost, Red," he brushes me off. "Get out of here before I change my mind."

With a wave, I head out of the alley, burner already in hand. It's already late, so I half expect that no one will pick up when I dial the number.

But luck is finally on my side.

"Hello?" an unfamiliar female voice says, the connection crackling in my ear.

"My name is Red. I just saw your ad in Rufin's paper."

THE CLIENT GAVE me the address of a 24-hour diner just outside of Newark. She was eager to meet at my earliest convenience.

I'd asked if she could be there in a few hours.

I could hardly believe it when she agreed.

Torn between celebrating my good fortune and being more suspicious of the coincidences involved in this job, I take a taxi to the diner and find myself walking across the vinyl floors at exactly three a.m.

At this hour, there's barely anyone sitting inside besides a couple of trucker types and an older woman who looks like she's fallen asleep in her booth. It makes my client very easy to spot.

Her eyes find mine the second I step into view.

She's young. Younger than me, even. Tan skin, dark eyes, and a beautiful mass of curls piled up on her head. Even in her nondescript hoodie and jeans, it's difficult for her not to stand out.

She looks about as surprised as I feel as I go to take my seat opposite her.

"Red?" she asks tentatively, though I don't think either of us needs the clarification.

"Rufin said you were new, but..." I let my words trail off.

She looks down at this, bashful, somehow, appearing even younger than a second ago. "I'm twenty-one."

"Right." I turn to wave the bored-looking server over. "So, what does a twenty-one-year-old need with a mercenary like me?"

The question hovers between us for a moment before the server appears, granting my potential client time to think up an answer. I order a milkshake in another attempt to put her at ease.

She smiles slightly and orders the same.

"I imagine this is a bit strange for you," she says once the server leaves us again. "It's strange for me too."

I wait patiently for her to gather her nerves, sitting back in my seat and trying to figure out who she could be. She has a slightly non-rhotic accent, but that's typical of this area. She's too tan to be Irish. She's too memorable to be Italian.

"My family...my father," she corrects herself. "Expects me to make an entrance into his society next week. I managed to delay it until I finished college, but now there's no way to get out of it."

"I'm guessing you're not debuting at the country club?" I deadpan.

She looks up at me then, biting at her bottom lip. "Are you Irish?"

I blink at her. "Is it the hair?"

"Rufin..." she trails off as two milkshakes are placed before us. There's a beat of silence while we both take a sip.

Just two young women enjoying a midnight treat, nothing to see here.

"Do I need to be Irish?" I ask carefully.

She shakes her head. "You'd just need to pose as my friend. Undercover, that is."

"You're worried about your father's society friends?"

"I trust my father's...friends to stay in line," she says. "I just know if anything were to go wrong, they would answer to him and not me. I want someone there who I can rely on to put me first."

Slowly, I begin to put the pieces together. "Hiring a beefed-up bodyguard to follow you around all night would be suspicious. Your Irish friend from college, however..."

"Exactly."

It's a smart enough move, one I would certainly consider should I ever find myself in her position. Nothing about the job seems too suspicious, and the woman seems too nervous to pull off some kind of setup.

I take another sip of my milkshake before getting down to business.

"Is it just your debut, then? Or will you need me for other events?" I ask.

"There might be a few in the future," she admits. "If this works and we can pull it off convincingly, that is."

"Where did we go to college?"

"Princeton."

My eyebrows raise at that. "Impressive. Studying what?"

"Bioengineering." She flushes modestly.

I let out a low whistle. "I was a lowly business major at Columbia."

Her eyes light up at this, and I instantly realize my mistake. "Really?"

Maybe I'm a bit rusty after all, sharing personal information like that. Fuck. She could find me now if she wanted to.

"It was a few years ago now." I try to cover up my fumble by redirecting the conversation. "Sorority sisters?"

She makes a face. "Roommates."

I almost laugh at her obvious disdain. "No 'Delta, Delta, Delta' for you in Princeton?"

"Those girls terrified me," she admits.

"Says the woman hiring a mercenary."

She weighs this up. "When you grow up with this stuff, it's strange how easy it is to forget it's not normal."

Her words strike a very particular chord, and I find myself swallowing down something hard lodged in my throat. Suddenly, I feel sorry for both of us. "Okay."

"Okay?"

"I'll do it."

"Shouldn't you ask me about payment?"

I give her a look. "Are you going to pay me?"

"Yes."

"Good, that settles that." I slide another burner across the table to her. "Contact me on this. All my details are already in there. You can keep calling me Red."

She takes the cell from me. "Red works."

"What should I call you?"

"I suppose you'll find out soon enough," she sighs, tucking a strand of dark hair behind her ear. "My name is Carmen. Carmen Rubio."

8

LEON

Amos Rubio might be a bigger thorn in my side than Mia Natali née Chiavari.

In the three days since I last saw my wife, I've been relentlessly throwing myself into my work, eager to distract myself from the festering wound of rejection she left behind.

Only to be pinned down by an altogether different problem.

"He's moved the shipment again," Dante reports to me in my office above the casino.

Max doesn't bother concealing his groan. "Surely, he's run out of dockyards by now."

"We're monitoring everything in Brooklyn." Dante flops down in the seat next to my second. "Teo's asking if you can double down here."

"We spent the last week searching for his new shipment. I don't have the men to double down again," I tell him. "How the hell did he find out we were on to him?"

Dante winces in a way that makes me think Teo has

been asking the same question. "He's always been a paranoid bastard."

"But this quickly?" I press.

He doesn't rise to the bait. "All we can do is start looking again."

"If he was importing merchandise into Manhattan, we would have found it by now," Max answers for us both. "Have you tried New Jersey?"

"The Irish don't want any part in this." Dante runs a hand through his dark hair.

"Staten Island?" Max says.

The three of us share a grimace.

With a sigh, I get to my feet. It's already late, and the lack of sleep I've been getting for the last few days is starting to weigh on me.

"Tell Teo I'll be at the old shipment site tomorrow to see if I can pick up on any clues as to where he might have moved to. But we can't spare the men to do anything more than keep an eye on our own dockyards."

"Have you got anyone who can join our search parties?" Dante says a little too carefully. "I think it would help Teo's gray hairs if we presented a united front."

I hear exactly what he's not saying. If there *is* a leak somewhere, the first place the Guild is going to point is at the Prince's Hand and, in all honesty, Vitale versa. The alliance might be formally signed, but it's far too new and fragile to sustain that kind of infighting.

United front it is.

"What about my gray hairs?" I mutter to myself.

Max sighs and stands up. "I can go. But I'm taking Saturday off. I'm fucking exhausted."

I throw my hands up in the air in comical disbelief.

"Since when did you get the idea you could set your own hours?"

"Since I've come home every night this week stinking of fish, asshole."

Dante throws us both an amused look before standing as well. "I'll get going, too. If there's an update before tomorrow, I'll call you, Leon, before you hit the shipment site."

Exhaustion hits me quite cruelly between the eyes. The last thing I want to do is scramble over to Brooklyn at some ungodly hour tomorrow morning, but I need to be at least seen doing my part by the Guild.

"Thanks." I get up as well. "Tell Teo to let me know if he has any more ideas about...united efforts."

Dante thinks about this for a moment. "Matching T-shirts?"

"Couples costumes!" Max clicks his fingers.

Dante smiles at him conspiringly. "Leonardo and Michaelangelo?"

"I was going to say Mario and Luigi. But you're right. Leon is more of a renaissance guy."

"I was thinking turtles."

"All right, get the fuck out of here," I half-yell at them, and they obediently skitter out of the room.

I'm still shaking my head as I lock up for the night. Simon is at the front desk as I leave. He offers me his usual nod of acknowledgment as I pass. His eyes are ever-assessing. I have no idea what he is thinking most of the time. Somehow, I find that comforting.

I know how I look. I know how much coffee he's brought me today to compensate for the lack of sleep that's so clearly etched itself on my face. I blame it on the new house, the new environment. The emptiness of it. The lack of...

The thought of going back suddenly stops seeming so appealing. For a long moment, I debate turning around and spending the rest of my evening lost on the casino floor.

It feels a lot more welcoming than returning to the brownstone alone.

But all this business with Amos Rubio...united efforts... Brooklyn bright and early in the morning, another sleepless night...I may well ruin whatever tentative progress we've already made if I can't even think clearly.

Begrudgingly, I step out into the night and head home.

It's with an odd sense of deja-vu that I ascend the front steps of the brownstone and walk inside. It's just another night, another empty house with nothing but Caravaggio for company.

I shouldn't feel alert. Shouldn't expect anything out of the ordinary. There's nothing *different* per se; it's just a feeling of *something*.

The house doesn't feel lonely. It feels like a home.

When I find Mia pacing the lounge, it's not unexpected.

Her hair is curled up into a bun. A few tendrils have fallen down to frame her face, perfectly out of place. She's so devastatingly pretty.

She freezes as I lean against the doorframe and cross my arms. I am absolutely not drinking her in like a man parched due to her lack of attention. "I never asked the other day, but how do you keep getting in here?"

This is apparently not what she expected me to say, as her mouth opens in a perfect little "O" shape.

"Would you believe me if I told you I stole the key from under the mat?"

"No, not really."

She doesn't elaborate any further. Not that I really expected her to.

"Can I get you a drink? Whiskey?" I ask instead, keeping my tone as neutral as possible.

"No."

Unyielding, frustrating woman.

With a sigh, I take a step further inside. She takes a measured step back away from me. Deliberate, overly cautious, like she's learned something from last time.

"This was a mistake," she says warily. "I should have gone to Teo."

A pang of unrestrained jealousy hits me out of nowhere, and I try desperately to rein it back in, focusing instead on the woman before me.

Mia looks concerned. Concerned enough to come back here, even after putting very clear boundaries between us last time.

She also looks, quite unfairly, beautiful. There's something about the night that suits her so perfectly. I think it's the darkness of her clothes and the way they complement her skin tone. She's a creature of secrets and shadows, whispers under bed sheets, the knife that you never expect until it's lodged in your heart.

I mentally chastise myself for getting so distracted. "Why would you go to Teo?"

"You going to pull the 'you don't belong to the Guild anymore' card on me?" she retorts.

"Do I have to?"

She considers me for a moment before dropping down on the couch. "I have a lead on Amos Rubio."

The silence that stretches between us constricts my

breathing. It's unseemly how quickly that name sets off all my internal alarms. For it to come out of Mia's mouth…

"How do you have a lead on Amos Rubio?" I say as evenly as I can.

Regardless of my effort for control, Mia clearly picks up on my anger. Her expression becomes more guarded and far more cold than before. "I met with a new client yesterday."

I close my eyes and breathe in and out twice.

"A new client."

"Yes."

"Someone who wanted to hire you as a mercenary," I clarify.

"Yes."

I'm suddenly very grateful she declined the drink. This is not the time to have a glass in my hand. "You weren't supposed to take on any work like that without consulting me."

"I can't remember that being a part of our marriage vows."

"You're being contrary on purpose."

She matches my tone entirely. A challenge. I usually love a challenge. "I've done everything else you wanted. You don't control me."

"You are purposefully putting yourself in danger in spite of my direct instructions. You were supposed to tell me."

"I'm telling you now."

"Jesus Christ!" I yell a little louder than necessary.

It makes her flinch. It's horrific to see. I want to snatch the words back from where they linger in the air between us.

I slowly, carefully take a seat as far from her as possible. "I'm sorry," I say instead.

She swallows hard. "I'm capable of making my own decisions. I know how to keep myself safe."

I bite my tongue to stop the protests that bubble up.

Logically, I know she can look after herself. I've seen her client list, read through her accomplishments. On paper, Mia is more than capable; she's effective...ruthless even.

It's just very different now that I know her, know all the places where she's soft and warm and wanting. The instinct to *protect* overwhelms every other rational thought.

"The only reason I'm telling you is because it's an opportunity the mafioso would kill for," she looks away. "That, and I need some help."

The admission takes me by surprise. "Okay. Let's hear it."

"Did you know that Amos Rubio has a daughter?" she says slowly. "Her name is Carmen. She just graduated from Princeton."

I stare at her for a long time. Amos' private life was one that neither the Guild nor the Prince's Hand had been able to gather any kind of information on. He was presumed to be widowed, but any reference to a child or children simply did not exist.

Both Isabella and Teo had tried to find information in the depths of the Cartel's encrypted files but became frustrated when they found that the kingpin was too old school for an electronic trail.

To prove her point, Mia indicates the sheets of paper in the middle of the coffee table. "I double-checked with the admissions office today. Amos Rubio paid her tuition in full."

I don't want to know how she managed to extract that

presumably *extremely* confidential information from the Princeton admissions office.

"How did your client know about this?" I ask, glancing warily at the evidence before me.

"My client *is* Carmen Rubio."

We stare at each other for what feels like an age.

Anyone else. *Anyone else.*

If Max had come to me with this, if Dante had. Hell, if that "retired" bastard Rocco Moretti had deigned to visit with this news, I would have cracked open the fucking champagne.

Why did it have to be Mia?

"You just happen to get contract work with the Cartel kingpin's daughter?"

"Yes."

"It's obviously a trap," I say, even though it doesn't quite make sense. Because nobody knows that Mia is my wife. Mia isn't known to be affiliated with *anyone.*

Mia seems prepared for this line of questioning, though. "That's what I thought, but this girl…Leon, she's so green. She barely has any idea what she's doing aside from the fact she needs help. Amos doesn't know that she's hiring me."

I ignore the way my name on her lips makes my heart clench. "Okay, so we let her hire someone else. You send your apologies and your recommendation. My second is new enough to New York. They won't look twice at him."

"That won't work," she protests. "She needs a woman, specifically. Someone who won't stand out at her side during a party. Besides, I've already made contact and connection. She trusts me."

"Then we get another woman to do it," I counter.

This makes Mia laugh sharply. "Who? Isabella? The

Cartel has a target on her back almost as big as yours! There isn't anyone else, not on this short notice."

I wish she wasn't right. God. I wish there was someone else.

"I'm not asking for your permission," she continues. "The party is on Saturday. I'm going to go. If you want to use this opportunity to your advantage, now is your chance to brief me on what you need."

Positive IDs on Amos' inner circle. Car registration numbers. Politicians and high society members with personal invitations. Hell, even a *look* into the man's office would at least confirm our theory that the man operates offline.

As a don, there's no way I can miss out on this. As a husband...

"You said you needed help?" I say, a safer topic.

This, inexplicably, makes her look away. There's a pretty little flush on her cheeks. "My...er...equipment is a little dated. I need to upgrade a few things, but I'm sort of out of work at the moment."

I blink at her, suddenly feeling quite blindsided. She's asking for *money*. My wife is worried about her finances. I would laugh if the whole thing wasn't entirely ridiculous.

My wallet is out a second later, and I hand her my black card without hesitation. "I should have given you one sooner."

"I don't need your charity." She stares at the card as if it somehow offends her. "I thought you might give me a forward for the information I manage to acquire at the party."

I reach for her hand and place the card in her palm, ignoring the way something in my soul sings at the physical contact. "I'm not paying my wife a 'forward'. This is your money now."

Very hesitantly, Mia curls her fingers around the card, barely brushing my hand as she does so. Her throat bobs as she swallows hard.

"Okay. What do you need?"

9

MIA

I descend the staircase of the brownstone on Saturday evening, still attaching a gold hoop to my ear. Late, late, late.

Leon messaged me to say my equipment had arrived this morning, but I'd lost the day compiling as much information as I could on the Rubios. By the time I'd shown up at the door, I was already behind schedule.

Carmen had texted me the address of her apartment so we could ride in together. It was halfway across town, and I had exactly eighteen minutes to get there.

"The camera took forever to charge," I say to the back of Leon's head—the man has apparently been pacing since I arrived. "I'll keep it plugged in on my way over and turn it on when I arrive."

"You've got the..." he turns just as I take the final two steps. My gold heels click along the wooden floor as I approach. "Um..."

I push my hair over my ear to conceal the earpiece and brush down my dress for good measure. It's a simple black number, with a long slit in the side that allows me some semblance of mobility.

"Um?" I press. I really am running late.

His eyes snap up to meet mine, his mouth a little wide. Was he just... "Tracker," he blurts out. "The tracking deVitale, did you manage to—"

I turn to my side to hoist up my dress a little to reveal the garter underneath. Knife, tracking deVitale, and three doses of GHB.

"Jesus fucking Christ," I swear I hear him mutter as my eyes snap up to his. By the time I look at him again, his back is straighter, his face unemotional.

"I'm on channel three." I indicate my ear before checking the slim, gold Cartier watch on my wrist. "And I'm late, so..."

"Right." Leon steps to one side, clearing his throat as I pass him. "I'll be here, keeping an eye on everything. Dante is–"

"A half mile away if I need an extraction, I know." I tap my foot impatiently. "Can I go?"

I don't miss the way Leon swallows, dark chocolate eyes taking me in unashamedly. I notice the whiteness of his knuckles as he clenches his fists. He doesn't like this, that much is obvious. But he's letting me go anyway.

"Be careful, Mia," he sighs.

A shiver runs down my spine at the soft caress of my name.

"I will."

"OH! AND HORSES," Carmen says as we walk up to the front door of the mansion in Bayswater.

The Cartel debutant is in a breathtaking golden gown, fiddling with the tiara resting on top of her beautifully defined curls. The headgear might have looked a little tacky on anyone else, but it's a simple, modern band that's definitely sporting a few diamonds and it suits her.

"Horses?" I repeat as I reach over to settle the tiara on her head, pushing away her fussing fingers.

She relents and allows me to help her. "I was a part of the equestrian team at Princeton. Do you ride?"

"No," I admit, taking a step back to admire my work. "But I would have come to see your shows. Dressage, right?"

Carmen nods eagerly, but thankfully, the tiara stays exactly where it should. She sighs and throws her hands out a little awkwardly. "How do I look?"

It's very hard not to feel a sense of fondness for the girl. Well, woman, really. She looks so nervous, yet there's a twinkle of excitement in her eyes, and that same enthusiasm is evident in the way she bounces on her heels slightly as if she can't quite stand still.

"You're going to knock them out," I tell her, not needing to lie even a little.

She'd confessed on the ride over that it'd been four years since she last saw most of these people. Back then, she'd barely been a footnote in the life of the Cartel, always kept behind closed doors, always just hidden from view.

Now, as I open the front door of the mansion for her, every single guest turns to take a look. Each seems more curious than the next to see how Amos' precious Princeton grad grew up.

Carmen stands for a moment in the foyer, looking more

than a little overwhelmed at the sudden attention. Not that I blame her. There must be fifty people ogling her right now.

"*I need faces,*" Leon suddenly murmurs in my ear. It's an unsettling feeling. He must have spent an ungodly amount of money on my gear. The clarity of the sound in my earpiece makes it seem as if he were standing right behind me.

I give myself a second to breathe, smile, and then approach the bewildered Carmen, casually looping my arm through hers. "Oh my God, Cammy! This place is gorgeous!" I gush, squeezing her arm twice.

One for bad, two for good. We'd decided in the car.

I make sure to look around at our audience, catching them with my concealed camera under the guise of admiring the extensive entrance hall.

I feel her instantly relax at my side. "You should see the ballroom." She tugs me forward. "Come on, I'll show you."

We natter on as Carmen leads me through the ground floor. We look for all the world like two excited women squealing about the grandeur of a party after four years of student living.

A couple of people stop us to congratulate Carmen. I make a mental note of their names and their faces as I quietly wait for my companion to politely thank them or regale them with a tale of late nights at the library and hard work paid off.

By the time we reach the ballroom, Carmen seems to have completely settled into her role. She's a natural at this, a huge smile on her lips despite the excruciating politeness.

"My Papi should be around here somewhere," she mentions as we begin to wander through the hall.

It's also magnificent, adorned with all the fixtures of

wealth one might find in some kind of castle. High ceilings, gallery feature walls, and humongous chandeliers are everywhere.

I let out a whistle as I take it all in, thoroughly distracted by what Carmen just said.

That is, until we come to a halt in front of a very large, very intimidating group of men. They part at the sight of Carmen, many wearing appreciative expressions as they appraise her. I try not to let my toes curl. No wonder she wanted private backup.

"Maji?" a deep voice calls out from the very center of the pack.

Before my very eyes, Amos Rubio steps forward.

It's strange because I've known about this man for so long. I've seen his half-blurred face in CCTV footage, been shown his mug shot from twenty-odd years ago. But I've never confronted him in person.

I think I imagined he'd be taller, this intimidating force of a man that has overshadowed the Guild for years. But in reality, he's just a normal man in an expensive suit. Tattoos creep out of his sleeves across his fingers. His dark hair shaved short.

His leathery skin wrinkles when he smiles at the sight of his daughter.

"You look beautiful," he says as he pulls her in for a tight embrace.

I watch with the reunion with a placated smile, trying to ignore the prickle of curious attention beginning to be directed my way.

"The one on the right, red tie. That's Ivan. We caught him on CCTV planting—"

"Who is this, Mija?" Amos Rubio pulls back from his

daughter to appraise me. It's a calculating look, but not one that seems overly suspicious.

I step forward with a bright smile, flicking my hair back as I hold out my hand. "Holly McDonald, sir. But everyone just calls me Red."

"Remember Papi? I told you she's my friend from school." Carmen rolls her eyes.

Then suddenly, I'm shaking hands with Amos Rubio. In the middle of his own house. Surrounded by the enemy.

"So pleased to meet you!" I lay it on a bit thick. "I owe your daughter a life debt, you know. She saved me from getting trampled to death by a rogue stallion back in Princeton."

To her credit, Carmen easily plays along. "I just nudged you out of the way," she says, words laced with false modesty.

Amos drops my hand, seemingly placated. "Carmen has a habit of bringing out loyalty in people. Did you also major in Bioengineering?"

"Red is a business major," Carmen answers for me.

This seems to capture his attention somewhat. "And what kind of business do you see yourself running?"

Hopefully, not a drug empire, Leon says in my ear.

I try to make the quirk of my lips at his words seem related to what I say out loud. "I actually make soaps and bathroom accessories. Bath bombs, ambience sprays, candles, that kind of thing."

Unintimidating, unassuming. A novelty. Don't look at me too hard.

It works. Amos instantly loses interest and refocuses on his daughter, telling her about all the people she needs to meet when he's expected to give a speech. I listen for the practical facts, but nothing interesting is said.

I'm also too distracted by the thought of strangling Leon for almost making me break my cover.

Finally, Carmen kisses her father and returns to my side, saying her goodbyes.

"Thanks so much for the invite!" I call over my shoulder toward Amos as we walk away.

"That went well!" Carmen chirps happily at my side. "He definitely bought it. Nice touch with the bath bombs."

"In another life, I think I would have made a pretty good artisanal soap maker," I say wistfully, earning a laugh from my client as we glide across the room again.

"Red's Apothecary has a good ring to it."

I'm about to reply when someone reaches for Carmen's arm. My knee-jerk reaction is to snatch at it, to yank them away from my charge. But I squash the urge quickly—there are far too many people in this room for theatrics.

"Carmen," he says, and my eyes snag on his red tie.

Carmen jolts slightly at the contact but seems to relax when she realizes who has caught her. "Ivan."

"Can I talk to you?" He's wearing a strained expression, dark eyes darting to me, then back to Carmen. "Alone?"

The debutant reaches for my hand, squeezing it twice. *One for bad, two for good.*

I take my cue gracefully. "Sure thing. I was just going to go find a bathroom. I'll see you in a bit, Cammy?"

"What are you doing? I need intel on Ivan."

I ignore him, wandering out of the ballroom and snagging a glass of fizzy alcohol from a waiter's tray as I pass by.

This might be my only chance to get away from Carmen

safely all night without jeopardizing my cover. I'm going to make the most of it.

When I enter the next room—a gorgeous conservatory-style dining hall—I make sure to stumble a bit, giggling as I right myself.

"Excuse me." I approach the closest couple I can find. "Do you know where...where...the er...bathroom is?"

Predictably, they both move out of the way as soon as the amber liquid from my glass slops lazily onto the floor.

"Oops," I mumble to their retreating figures. "I'll go find someone to clean that...up."

"What are you doing?"

I want to tell him that I'm collecting a few eyewitnesses to the drunken redheaded friend making a fool of herself, who can place me stumbling around the ground floor if anyone were to ask.

I dip out with another laugh and beeline it for the staircase I saw on my way in. I keep up my drunken act as I ascend. No doubt there are more than a few eyes at the party keeping a lookout for suspicious behavior.

But as I make it to the landing, there doesn't seem to be anyone who follows me.

"You don't have time for this. Carmen will be looking for you soon."

"You wanted information. I'm getting you information," I hiss back as I make my way down the empty corridor. Pausing at a few doors to peer inside.

The first few places I check are entirely empty. Bathrooms, a long lounge that looks over the front driveway, a library of some kind.

It's not until I'm halfway down the hallway that I begin to hear voices.

"... has already been moved too many times."

I slow my pace, lingering by a cracked open door to try and listen in.

"I don't care," another voice replies. "Move it again."

"There's nowhere else, not unless you want to go private."

"Then go private."

"It'll cost you a lot of hush money."

"Money I have. What I don't have is a safe landing spot for the shipment. Make the fucking call."

In my ear, I hear Leon's sharp intake of breath. *"Holy shit."*

I take that as permission to leave, hurrying back toward the staircase before anyone can notice me missing.

Only to run straight into someone at the top of the stairs. "Oh! Excuse me," I say automatically.

Hands dig into my shoulders as they stand me back up. "The hell are you doing up here?"

I blink up. Red tie. Ivan.

"Get the FUCK out of there."

"Looking for the bathroom." Fuck, fuck, fuck. "Have you seen Carmen? I was chatting with this gorgeous blonde guy earlier...hey, do *you* know if he's single? Tall, dark suit. Fuck-me-eyes?"

He shoves me to one side, clearly unamused by the conversation. "The upper floors are off-limits. Please bear that in mind as you enjoy the rest of the party, Miss McDonald."

"Call me Red!" I sing back as I make my descent, purposefully stumbling once or twice, trying to cover for the fact my voice is shaking.

10

LEON

The video feed cuts out like it's fucking amateur night right as Ivan confronts Mia.

It takes everything within me not to punch a hole through my monitor.

"FUCK!" I shout into the empty house.

Vaguely, I'm aware that it had been a smart decision to stay away from the Cartel's mansion tonight. If anyone discovered me, Mia's cover would have been blown.

But right now, I'm struggling to see a single merit in this line of thinking. I should be storming the place right now. I should get into my car and drive and drive until I have her in my sights. I need to make sure that she's okay. Screw everything else.

All I have is a pathetic little pulsing dot on my screen. It's a tracker, not a heart monitor, but I still watch it as if it indicates a sign of life.

I wonder if I can convince her to wear a heart monitor next time.

My hand instantly begins to pull on my own hair, sharply tugging me back to reality.

Next time? There shouldn't have been a *first* time.

I should never have agreed to this. I should never have allowed her to put herself in danger, should never have asked her to go looking for more information.

I should have charged the fucking camera for her.

Now, there's nothing I can do but wait. I think I might go insane.

I swipe up on my phone screen and dial Dante.

"I've lost eyes on her," I bark as soon as he picks up. I hope that the strain in my voice is less apparent down the phone line.

It had been necessary to tell him about the marital arrangement with Mia, although from his subdued reaction, I'd say he already had an idea of what was going on. After all, he did sign the alliance papers.

"Shit," Teo's second responds instantly. "I'm not spotting any unusual movement. Rotation of staff has been consistent at this point, but I won't know if there's been any disruption to their shift pattern for another…three minutes and twenty seconds."

"What if she doesn't have three minutes?"

Dante shuffles on the other end of the line. "What did you last see?"

"Ivan. He'd found her somewhere she shouldn't have been."

"Do you think she can handle herself?"

The question dangles in the air between us. I don't answer, not entirely trusting myself to say something rational.

"Leon. It's your call. I can go in and get her out, but I

need you to be positive that she can't deal with this on her own."

If it were anyone else, I'd give them a grace period. That would be the smart thing to do. To trust my men to make the right decisions and only jeopardize the mission as a last resort.

But Mia isn't just some Prince's Guild lackey. She's my *wife*.

God, the word barely has any significance between us. I have no right to claim it. But right now, I can feel myself curling around the word protectively, possessively. I feel like some kind of dragon curling around a precious, sparkling gem.

That one. There, in the stunning black dress and the garter that is slightly too high up her perfect thigh. She's mine. She's in danger.

My wife, my wife, my wife.

I shake myself, trying to strangle the thought. "Tell me as soon as the rotation changes."

It's the right call. Just not an easy one.

Dante stays on the line while we wait in silence. My eyes never stray from that pulsing dot on my screen.

Then.

"Shift as normal, Leon. No disruption inside."

The breath I was holding knocks through my ribs as I let it out. "Right."

"Again, it's your call, but…"

"Continue to monitor the situation as planned," I say with a sigh.

"Copy that." Dante doesn't immediately hang up as expected. "She's…a force to be reckoned with. She'll be fine, Leon."

I don't take too much comfort from his words, but I swallow a scolding response all the same. "Update me if anything goes awry."

I'M in the kitchen when the front door opens. The very picture of calm and collected.

If you ignore the fact I've been tracking her little dot on my phone for hours now.

The tension in my shoulders releases a bit more with every centimeter it beats back toward my location. It's not a heartbeat, I remind myself. But she's coming anyway. Soon, she will be home and safe.

Of course, someone could have intercepted her and taken the tracking deVitale. But Dante called to say he was following her back to Carmen Rubio's apartment, where she dropped off the debutante without any issues.

Dante was likely parked outside now, watching as Mia entered the house. I make a mental note to thank Teo for letting me borrow his second.

"Leon?" her voice calls out.

"In here."

There's the clicking of heels on the wooden floor, and then...

...and then she's there.

She's still unfairly stunning in that sinful black dress, still holding herself tall. Even her makeup seems to have stayed exactly in place.

I bury my fingernails into the palms of my hands to stop myself from reaching for her. Something primal within me needs to do more than see, to *touch,* to make sure that she's okay. That there's not even a hair out of place on her head.

Words don't feel like enough, but I force myself to settle for them instead. "Are you all right?"

"Yes, fine," she brushes me off, uncaring, unaware of the knots coiling in my stomach. "Did I get everything you needed?"

I swallow. I'm still looking, still assessing every visible inch of her. "The camera cut off."

"Oh. Sorry, I should have charged it more."

"It wasn't your fault."

"Leon?"

"Hm?" My eyes snap to meet hers, looking away from analyzing her preference to weight bear on her left leg. Did she always do that? Or did she injure herself at the party?

"Don't...take this the wrong way, but...are you alright?"

A bark of laughter escapes my lips. *Me?* I shake my head in disbelief. "We can debrief in the morning if you're tired. I caught enough of the evening to begin making progress."

"Okay. I'll go then."

No, no. No. I've only just got her back. She's only just become *safe*.

"You have a room here," I blurt out. "If you want it. Save you the trouble of getting across town."

Please, please. Please.

I feel so tightly coiled. If I make one wrong move, I'll completely spring into chaos. I won't be able to let her go. I can't let her leave this house. Not until this feeling ends, not until I'm *sure* she's okay.

"I suppose that makes sense." She bites her lip. "Will you be coming up?"

Her cheeks instantly redden as I look up at her in alarm.

"I mean, you said you were going to begin making progress. I was wondering if you intending to sleep tonight," she corrects herself hurriedly.

"There's not much point. Usually, after something like this, I'm a little...pent up." It's not even a lie, although this level of anxiety is definitely new. "But you should rest."

She nods and starts to leave, only to linger in the doorway, hesitating.

There's something she's not saying. She must have been hurt, after all. They must have gotten to her. They must have threatened her...

"Are you sure you're alright?" I press, unable to keep the desperation out of my tone this time.

"Yes. It's just that I'm...um...I started ovulating."

Her words are like a master key, making quick work of all the emotions I've had restrained in the back of my mind. "What?"

"I got the notification on the ride over and—"

I'm like a moth to a flame. Her eyes go wide with something indiscernible as I make my approach.

My hands instantly reach for her face to hold her there, and finally, there's the touch I've been craving. It's an overindulgence to examine her like this, checking her head, her jaw, her neck, hands skimming over skin just to make sure.

"I'm not tarnished goods." She breaks me from my spell with the harshness of her words. "Do you really need to inspect me like this?"

My movements immediately freeze up. "I'm not—"

"Can we just get this over with? It's been a long night."

She's not looking at me. I need her to look at me.

"Yes, it has." The words come out more tenderly than I

intended, but it works. Those huge green eyes look up at me, and I watch as her mouth drops into a slight "O".

I could get lost in those eyes and just hold her close until morning breaks us apart. I'd be satisfied with only that.

But her eyes lower to my lips and suddenly, the possibility of *more* sets everything within me alight.

I could have her right here on the kitchen floor, pushed up against the door frame, over the counter like I'd imagined only a few days ago. I could. It would be…hard to justify, with comfortable beds right upstairs. But I *could* do it.

"What are you—"

But I *can't* explain, so instead, I sweep up her legs and pick her up, bridal style. The irony isn't lost on me, just buried under the overwhelming sensation of her body pressed firmly against mine.

"Put me down!" she half stutters the words.

"You must be tired." The excuse sounds feeble as I move us toward the stairs, up toward my bedroom.

"I don't need you to manhandle me."

"Don't you?"

I can feel her tense in my arms. "I can walk."

"I can carry you."

She protests some more, but I ignore every word until my bedroom door slams shut behind us.

I set her down somewhat gingerly. I assume that's what the irritated frown on her face is for. But the expression does nothing to mar her loveliness. That fucking dress she's wearing might be the death of me.

She stands there, defiant, arms crossed, eyebrow raised, waiting for me. *Are we doing this then?* she seems to ask without the words leaving her mouth.

In response, I remove my cufflinks. It's a formal gesture that I follow with the unbuttoning of my shirt.

I don't miss the way her eyes rake over my bare chest as soon as it's revealed to her. I let the smugness into my smirk as I take a step toward her.

"This...off. Take this off," I demand as I circle around her, lifting the strap of her dress for a moment with my fingers. There are no bruises or marks on the backs of her arms or shoulders.

She does so carefully, letting the dress pool at her feet. She's remarkably confident, almost pragmatic.

There's nothing beneath the dress but the garter she flashed at me earlier.

"What the fuck," I hiss, hands already reaching out to trail down her sides. I rake over every inch of my skin. No bruises, no marks. She's fine. She's fine. She's fine.

She swallows. "The dress was tight. You could see the panty lines through the fabric."

"You walked into that den of vipers looking like that with *nothing* on under your dress?" I growl as I come around back to her front.

"I had no intention of letting them know that," she shoots back, jaw set stubbornly. It's so sharp, yet it makes me want to kiss it...all of it.

My lips seek hers out immediately at the thought. Drawing her close by the back of the neck, I press my mouth against that stubbornness, eliciting a small gasp from her lips. "May I remind you that you are married."

Fingers press tightly into my arms, holding me in place. Encouraging me on.

"I don't hear my husband complaining."

The hands trailing down her skin pause between her

legs, where there is nothing preventing me from palming her sensitive nakedness.

Her gasp comes out as more of a moan. The sound is delicious and instantly goes straight to my cock.

"He's not," I whisper up her jaw.

For all her restraint, confidence, and pragmatism, it's Mia who moves first.

In a flash, her arms are locked around my neck, holding me down to her level so that she can press her lips against mine.

It's a filthy, filthy kiss. All teeth and tongue scraping against my own, drawing out hot, panting breaths from us both. I want all of it, need all of it. Every movement is such perfect evidence of her well-being; it soothes something deep within my soul.

My hand remains between her thighs, giving her something to grind upon as we battle for dominance. I practically whine in her mouth at her desperate thrusts.

She desires this; she desires *me*.

And fuck, if that doesn't tear me apart and unleash something entirely primal within me. I feel it in the way my fingers dig into her waist, possessively.

Mine, mine, mine.

I feel it in the strain of my pants, the way my teeth gorge themselves on her neck. Claiming, marking.

Mine, mine, mine.

"If you don't fuck me soon, I will bite off your fucking ear," she whispers far too close to the offending appendage.

Her voice is delirious in her desperation, a perfect match for my own feelings as I push a finger through the slickness between her thighs.

There's a cry and then, "Not that."

I ignore her, coating my finger before pushing it against her opening. She immediately slumps against me as I press it into her.

"Not again...not..." Her voice is strangled, barely indistinguishable from her groans. "Just fuck me, please."

But it's intoxicating the way she crumbles under the rhythm of my hand, like I'm the only thing holding her up. It's so vulnerable, it's so unlike the woman I have begun to get used to having in my life. No one gets to see her like this but me. It's all *mine*.

"I want you to enjoy this." I nuzzle into the side of her hair. "I want you to be able to take me comfortably."

"F...f-fuck that," she hisses.

I'm so distracted by the way she starts quivering that I don't notice her arm reaching down to snatch my hand away. She gives me no time to retaliate, slipping out of my grip entirely and moving over to the bed.

"Fuck me. Now." She looks angry. Fiery. Desperate. Her lips are swollen with the feverish kisses she just adorned my body with.

How can I deny her a goddamn thing?

I strip out of my pants immediately, my cock already thick and hard in my hand. I allow myself a stroke as I look down at her. Then another, as I reach the side table for the lube.

"I said, *now*," she half-yells as I take my time coating myself thoroughly.

When I return to her, I place my spare hand over her mouth. "Demanding little thing, aren't you?"

She glares at me over my hand, green eyes half-clouded with lust as I align myself at her entrance.

"No complaints about entering a den of vipers, but as

soon as you need something from me, well..." I push into her, barely past the tip.

My heart shudders at the sight of her eyes rolling back, her moan smothered by my fingers.

"It's maddening." It takes considerable effort to get the words out. "No regard for your own safety. Even now, you want it rough, don't you?"

Her back arches as I push all the way to the hilt.

"Listen to me closely." I withdraw, only to slam back into her again. This time, the sound she makes escapes my fingers. "I'm the only one who gets to be rough with you."

I slam into her again, and my vision begins to blur. "You don't take risks with anyone else."

Her legs tremble with the effort to meet my next thrust, driving me even deeper. "And you're going to start wearing a fucking heart rate monitor."

Teeth bite into my hand as I lose all semblance of control. Her fingers scrape down my back, making her own marks on my skin. Dear God, do I love it. I love that she's claiming me as I've claimed her.

I love the way her tightness around my cock gives me the most excruciating pleasure I've ever known.

I love that she's here and safe and writhing beneath me. The only bruises and markings on her body are the ones that I've put there.

I feel it when her body clenches, when the spasms of her orgasm hit, and the most beautiful sound erupts from her mouth. I could listen to it forever, I could so easily stay with her like this, fall into...

My orgasm hits with brutal force and unnerving clarity. As I gaze upon the stars in my own eyes, the ones that cast her in an ethereal sort of softness, the pressure in my chest becomes too much.

This is too much. All of it, these feelings—the way she feels—is all too much.

Fuck.

I wrench my mouth from her skin, from where I could taste her sweat and desire, and push myself away.

It's done. I've done what was needed. I can't keep feeling this way.

Because it feels far too much like vulnerability. It feels too much like a weakness to be exploited by my enemies. It feels too much like clouded judgment.

I would have jeopardized the mission tonight for her in a heartbeat.

She moans out her protest as I yank myself out of her, but I keep putting the inches between us. Clawing away from that soft, raging thing that threatens to consume me whole.

It feels like an *obsession*.

Unnatural, unhealthy, unwarranted obsession. I want to lock the doors and never let her leave this room again.

My breath comes out in short pants as I try to gather my willpower. Every breath of distance between us gives me a new sense of clarity. I cling to it, pulling myself away and off the bed.

"Leon?" She looks up at me in half-delirious confusion, blankets pulled haphazardly over her perfect body.

It would be easy to close the distance again, soothe the worry of her brow, tease a hand through her hopelessly tangled curls. But it's too dangerous a path. I can't fuel this obsession anymore.

"You can sleep here tonight," I manage to choke out in a level tone. "We can debrief in the morning."

I turn to leave, grabbing my discarded clothes from the floor as I do.

"Are you...walking away from me right now?"

The betrayal in her voice is the hardest thing to stomach, and when I reach the bedroom door, the bile tastes rancid in my mouth. "There was nothing in our vows that specified cuddling."

I close the door behind me before she has a chance to respond.

11

MIA

The morning debrief is perhaps the most awkward thing I've ever experienced in my life.

Mainly because Leon is doing his very best to ignore what happened last night. But also, because it's hard not to feel like a prized mare when your so-called husband won't look you in the eye.

"Are you sure Ivan said nothing else to you?" he asks me again from across the living room. I notice that he's a safe distance away.

I can see the irony in our role-reversal. It used to be me keeping him at arm's length. Now it seems that he can't get far enough away from me.

Honestly, it just feels like I have some kind of virus he's trying to protect himself from.

"For the last time. He just sent me on my way." I slump back into the couch, squinting at the sunlight peeking in through the window. "Why are you so interested in this Ivan guy anyway?"

If I wasn't already in a bad mood, mornings always bring

out the worst in me. I ran a bar for years. My days rarely started before noon for years and years.

"It's none of—"

"None of my concern, got it. Only it is a bit, because he knows my face now, doesn't he?"

Leon narrows his eyes at me, but I don't back down. "Then don't give him an excuse to see your face again."

"So what? I'm just supposed to just sit on my ass until Carmen reaches out again?"

"Exactly."

"Well, this has been productive," I say sarcastically as I stand, desperately trying to ignore my aching thighs. "I assume you're satisfied that I've fulfilled my wifely duties?"

He doesn't respond. Doesn't even look at me.

Is he embarrassed? Ashamed? I can't find any sympathy either way.

"I'm going home, then."

He doesn't stop me as I leave. I'm not sure if I want him to. I'm not sure how I feel about him at all.

I think the sex has really messed with me. The euphoria of pulling off the infiltration of the Cartel mixed with his protective...no, *possessiveness,* in bed really fed into my delusions of whatever this thing is between us.

Which is hilarious because there isn't a *thing* between us. Not with the man who threatened my father's life so I would marry him. Not with the man whose only interest in me starts and ends with my capacity to bear his children.

Sure, he always touched me like I mattered. Looked at me like he was trying to burn the image into his memory. Held me close and whispered things that still make my heart race just thinking about them.

At least, it had felt that way, until he'd jumped off the

bed and ran away from me like he couldn't bear the sight of me.

So, logically speaking, there's nothing for me even to be upset about, really. Because there's no *thing,* and there will never be a *thing,* because he's an asshole who doesn't even have the decency to stay the night with me.

The week that follows the debrief is dreadful, mainly because I'm tearing my hair out due to the sheer boredom of having absolutely nothing to do. I'm not even fully able to enjoy doing nothing because of the guilt of sitting around and doing nothing.

Cas calls at least once a day, and I meet her and baby Cory for coffee one afternoon. I pointedly refuse to talk about Leon the entire time, and Cas has the good sense to ramble on about things like pre-K and growth spurts.

Things I probably should be noting down for the not-so-distant future.

Except the thought of having a child feels as distant as the moon to me. I can't connect with it anymore than I connect with the idea of Leon being the father of my children.

My father visited once to deliver a belated wedding present—a gold necklace he claimed was an heirloom of some kind, but I wouldn't put it past him to pawn some expensive shit off on me in case I was short on cash.

Not that I am, technically, short of cash these days. Although the black credit card still sits unused in my purse.

There's also been no contact from Carmen beyond the thank you text she sent twenty minutes after I dropped her off at her place after the party. She's said at the door that she'd reach out when she needed me again.

Which also means I can't take on any more mercenary

jobs, because I might be needed by the Cartel debutant at the drop of a hat.

No *Candelabra*. No mercenary work. No Guild.

No Leon Natali.

I'm close to plucking out my own eyelashes on the evening of the eighth consecutive night alone in my tiny little studio apartment.

Which is why, I suppose, I call him.

"Are you all right?" He picks up on the second ring, sounding somewhat breathless.

"No."

"Where are you?"

I want to roll my eyes. "I'm dying of boredom."

There is a pause where I can hear the great Leon Natali let out a sigh of frustration. "How did you get this number?"

"How did you know it was me calling?" I counter.

"What do you want, Mia?" His voice is sharp, impatient. I wonder, vaguely, how much progress he's made on the Cartel since I collected the intel from the party.

"Something to stop me from crawling up the walls."

There's a beat of silence. "I don't see how this is my problem."

"It's your fault I don't have a job anymore," I argue back. "I used to have career prospects, you know, before you went and decided that you wanted me to pump out a bunch of—"

"YES, all right. I get it. Fuck."

"Just give me something," I hesitate before adding a softer word. "Please."

"There might be something."

"Whatever it is, yes."

Leon ignores me. "Teo said he once asked you to oversee

a casino in Brooklyn. Is that something you might still be interested in?"

"You want me to work for the Prince's Hand?" I say, a little taken aback. I hadn't considered the Prince's Hand casinos as a potential career path, but they were the main source of income for my new mafioso.

"Yes and no, it's an, er...collaboration project to showcase unity between the two Italian factions. His idea. Brooklyn location, Prince's Hand branding."

I bite my lip slightly. It would be a lie to say I hadn't thought about it since Teo originally proposed the idea. Managing an entertainment establishment was one of the few (legal) things for which I was actually qualified.

"Don't you think it's a risk? Someone might start paying attention to me," I mumble. "I don't want to blow my cover with Carmen."

"It's still under construction, so you wouldn't need to go to the site. Plus, you were Teo's entertainment manager. I don't think many would think twice about you being a part of the process."

Good enough for me. "I'll do it."

"Can you be at a meeting in an hour?"

THE ADDRESS IS a tall office building, the bottom floors comprising vast open-plan rent-a-desk spaces. The text Leon sends, however, guides me to a private meeting room several stories up.

The doors I pass by on my way contain large, corporate-style meeting rooms, so I half expect an entire committee to be sitting around the table.

So it's quite a surprise to see that only one person is waiting for me.

More of a surprise that it's my sister-in-law.

It's even more of a surprise that *she* doesn't seem that shocked to see me.

"Mia," the beautiful blonde greets me with a sarcastic little smile. Her quintessentially Italian features make a mockery of my own fading tan and Irish-red hair. She's perfectly presentable in her long Gucci boots and cashmere sweater.

God, I hate her.

"Isabella." I pointedly maintain eye contact so she doesn't glance down at the chucks falling apart on my feet. "I didn't know you'd be here."

"Didn't my brother tell you? It's a collaboration project."

It's condescending and boorish, and I wish I had had the foresight to bring a knife so we could settle this tension the way that both of us is itching to do.

Of course, she's here. Of course, this was the project he'd put me on.

"Please," I say instead. "It's clearly a WAGs project. Nice and safe away from prying eyes."

Her eyes narrow at that. "I should call Cas, then! See if she's up for a bit of fun."

Something cool and possessive stirs within me. Cassandra has been my friend since childhood. What kind of claim does Isabella Vitale have to her?

It's just playground tactics, I realize, with a start. And actually, I have no interest in playing.

"Are we doing this or not?" I say as I take a seat, not needing to feign my exhaustion as I look over some of the documents sprawled across the table before her.

Isabella eyes me cautiously before clearing her throat. "I've taken the liberty of printing off the floor plans for us. I think you'll find it all quite satisfactory. I've spent my entire life in casinos."

I glance at the paper she indicates. "And I've spent my entire life with the Guild. They're going to hate this."

"What are you talking about? These designs are perfect."

"The foyer is just a Prince's Hand logo."

"All our casinos have this style of foyer." She bares her teeth when she smiles.

"The design needs to be more subtle. This is like putting a statue of the Celtics in the entrance of Mia Square Garden." I pause for a second. "And they're not your casinos anymore, *Mrs. Vitale*. You married into the Guild."

Her lip twitches. "My brother already approved—"

"My *husband* asked me for my insight on this, so I'm giving it to you," I snap back.

Isabella sucks on her teeth. "You really wanna play this game with me?"

"No!" I say, exasperated. "I don't. I just want to get this over with so I can go back to my fucking apartment and be fucking miserable in fucking peace. This was a terrible, terrible idea."

I go to stand, but Isabella gets up with me. "Wait."

"What?"

"Neither of us wants to work on this."

I give her a long look. "No kidding."

"So, how about we just call a truce? Let's just...start again, shall we?" Isabella suddenly looks about as tired as I feel. "I'm still trying to get my head around the fact that it's *you* of all people who..."

She doesn't finish the sentence. She doesn't need to.

"The point is," she recovers after a moment, "I care about my brother. A lot. And Cas says you're a good person, but the thing is, I'm not sure if *I know* that's true. So you're really going to need to prove yourself to me."

"Are you seriously giving me the shotgun talk right now?"

"Yes," she says, unwavering. "Because my brother *is* a good person. And if you hurt him, Mia. I swear to God—"

My phone suddenly begins to ring. Which I'm sure I should probably completely ignore right now, given the circumstances.

Except it's my burner. And there's only one number on that phone.

"Excuse me," I mutter as I pull it out.

"I wasn't finished!"

"Bigger fish, Mrs. Vitale." I hold a finger up to silence her as I put it to my ear. "Carmen Rubio! It's been a while."

Isabella's face is absolutely priceless as she recognizes the name.

"Red!" A cheerful voice comes down the line. "I was just wondering, are you around this weekend?"

I look directly into Isabella's eyes, so like her brothers, as I reply. "For you, I'm free as a bird."

12

LEON

A tech-bro's beachfront villa. Practically a glorified frat house.

That's where my *wife* is going in denim short shorts and a backwards baseball cap. Both of which look entirely indecent on her.

The hat, because it pulls her hair from her face in a way that stops it from falling around her features with its usual heart-stopping softness. The shorts, because they are completely and utterly distracting and leave nothing to the imagination.

Not that I need to imagine, I try desperately to reassure myself. But there's an angry possessiveness inside me that a week's worth of distance has done nothing to subdue.

"Just...be careful, all right?" I ask as she leaves.

She doesn't look at me or bother responding as she steps out the door of the brownstone. That much I probably deserve after our previous spat about the pros and cons of heart rate monitors.

Mia wouldn't wear one. I tagged her anyway. She found it and threw it at my face.

I run a hand through my hair, suddenly wondering if it would be entirely unprofessional to start drinking.

It was inevitable that I would see her again, of course. But somehow, I'd managed to delude myself into just not thinking about it.

My insane workload was entirely to blame for this. The breakthrough we had had to search private dockyards, thanks to the information Mia had obtained, led to the very successful extraction of the Cartel's merchandise.

Now Teo and I were together on a near-daily basis to form plans to best utilize Amos Rubio's sudden loss of revenue.

My phone rings and I answer it as I return to my office, which is already set up for total surveillance tonight.

"She's arrived. Carmen Rubio just got in her car," Max reports immediately.

It's a reassurance to have him working on this with me. Unlike Dante, my second seems to inherently understand why I prefer to be constantly updated.

Despite not formally knowing who Mia is to me, he was quick to pick up on my anxiety around her involvement. I'd called her a mercenary for hire. Max hadn't even blinked when he gave me the concealable heart rate monitor.

A nice gesture if it didn't now lay broken on the floor.

"They're just talking," he continues.

I get a sickening sense of deja-vu as I watch Mia's pulsing red dot pause for a moment at the location.

Ivan had contacted Carmen to negotiate a small deal with a few of their higher-paying clientele. If I had to put money on it, I'd say it was an initiation for the debutant.

Clearly, these Silicon Valley wannabes emphasized discretion, and Carmen just happened to be perfectly cast to show up at one of their parties.

This meant that, once again, Mia would be playing the role of ditzy-soap-making-business-college-buddy.

And I hated it more than I could really express.

"They've just set off," Max interrupts my thoughts. "ETA forty-three minutes."

He will follow them the entire way, park at the neighboring beach villa, and keep tabs on the entire evening, reporting back to me with any progress or mishaps. He was instructed to intervene the second I gave the order.

De-ja-fucking-vu.

All I can do is stand here and wait. Wait forty-three minutes for them to arrive. Wait an hour or so for the interaction to last. Wait another forty-three minutes back and then...and then wait for Mia to come home.

Come back to *my* home. Not ours. Where she will, undoubtedly, give me the cold shoulder for the heart rate monitor thing. Or for setting her up on a project with my sister thing. Or for the walking out after sex thing.

It's just all one big fucking mess, really.

And all I can do is wait. Wait and wait, and go crazy waiting. Pacing and pacing and waiting and waiting and not being there to help if anything goes wrong because I'm too busy waiting.

I don't know when I leave the brownstone. Don't exactly know when I get into my car, a bag of surveillance gear and sniper rifle placed carefully in the trunk.

If it takes Mia forty-three minutes to get there, driving safely to keep her client safe, it takes me half that time.

"Max," I say into my phone as I pull into the neighboring beach house. "Change of plan."

I REALLY, really, truly hate those shorts.

The problem with looking at them from a high vantage point through a scope, is that with a small nudge of my hand, I can see every bastard she passes turn around to do a double take.

And the thing is, I've never really had a problem with a twitchy trigger finger until now.

She's standing outside by the goddamn infinity pool (did I mention how much I hate tech-bros) with an arm casually draped over Carmen's shoulders. She sips a beer from the bottle and nods at something Ivan says.

The older man might have looked a little out of place, but the company of the two women offsets the intimidating set of his shoulders and gang tattoos. No one around them has even spared them a second glance.

Except the bastards looking at her shorts.

Eventually, a guy comes out to meet them. He's tan, with reddish hair. Too young to be a millionaire—not that I can really talk, but at least I don't wear my wealth like he does, by buying tacky designer clothes and flaunting the labels like some kind of walking billboard.

The new money big shot says a few words to Ivan and gestures for the group to follow him inside.

When Carmen trails after him happily, Ivan pauses to stop Mia. There's a brief argument, a stalemate. *He doesn't want her to come along.* Then Carmen reappears, loops her arm through Mia's, and the three of them walk back inside as if that settles it.

For the time I don't have eyes on them, I feel something akin to terror begin to seep into my bones.

I can see the room they're going to arrive in. It's perfectly adjacent to the one I'm currently sitting in. The floorplans of the two beach houses mirror each other exactly.

Inside are three men sitting around an office. I've clocked them all already and sent their pictures to Max, but they're not affiliated with anyone we know. Just a bunch of kids playing at drug lords who got in a bit too deep with an actual kingpin.

They shouldn't be a threat.

Yet, when the door opens, and Mia, Carmen, Ivan, and the walking billboard walk in, my heart still stammers in my chest.

I absently grab at the headphone dangling from my neck and tune in.

"...you could make it!" One of the men, presumably the one with his back to me, is saying.

"Let's skip the preamble," the one by the door with a neck tattoo says. Who is...for fuck's sake, also staring at Mia's ass.

"If you were in such a rush, why did you make us wait downstairs for half an hour?" Ivan replies.

"It's such a gorgeous house," Carmen speaks over him, cheerful and light. "Maybe we could come back sometime when we don't need to talk business."

Neck Tattoo softens a bit, tearing his eyes from Mia for a full ten seconds to appreciate the other woman. "You and your friend are welcome whenever you like."

"Good! Everything has been so dreary since we lost the

last shipment," she continues in (what I'm suddenly realizing is) a very *fake* Valley Girl voice. "This place seems so much more fun."

"What shipment?"

"We'll get another in a few days." She rolls her eyes as if this is just a minor inconvenience, and they're all being dramatic. "There's nothing to worry about."

"You don't have the merch?" the guy with his back to me says.

Ivan takes a step forward. Mia subtly moves closer to Carmen. "This time next week, you'll all be out of freaking minds you're so high. What's the problem?"

"The problem is we already paid for it," Billboard Guy says, pushing past him to stand with his friends.

"And you'll get it," Carmen insists. "Jesus, calm down a little. I thought you guys were cool."

Her indignation, surprisingly, seems to placate them. If I'd known conflicts could be solved by a scolding from a pretty young woman, I would have hired Carmen years ago.

"When will it get here?" Billboard Guy asks.

"We'll be in contact before Wednesday," Ivan confirms.

"And until then?" Neck Tattoo says, leering at Carmen. "How am I supposed to entertain myself?"

His arm reaches out to touch the debutant, but Mia is on him like a flash.

"You want to try that again?" she says pleasantly as she twists his arm around in her hand.

He smirks back at her and pulls her in close. My skin is burning hot as my trigger finger itches and itches. "You jealous, sweetheart? Don't worry, you can entertain me too."

Slap.

Carmen Rubio shakes out her stinging hand—the imprint of which is now on Neck Tatoo's face.

I'd be impressed, except...

"What the actual fuck? You crazy bitch!"

...she just entirely blew her Valley Girl act. Whatever little bubble of calm Carmen had managed to wrangle out of the situation bursts in an instant.

Billboard Guy's hand disappears into his jacket. The quiet guy in the corner straightens up. The guy with his back to me reaches beneath the desk.

Ivan doesn't give them a chance to do anything.

Bang, bang, smash.

Three bullets: one for the quiet guy in the corner, one for Billboard Guy. One that was intended for the guy at the desk, but instead smashes through the window behind him.

I don't bother watching how that plays out.

Mia shoves Neck Tattoo against the wall.

"Back down, Carmen," Mia barks at her client, who obediently moves into the corner of the room and out of the fray. "St-..t...-right?"

She says something else, but the comms line crackles before sputtering out completely. Shit.

I watch as she pins him down with one hand, and a knife materializes in her other. The blade is at his neck in an instant, but not quick enough to keep him from wrangling an arm free.

You would think, in a life-or-death situation, the bastard would use the opportunity to his advantage. Shove the lethal woman away from him, pry the blade from her hand, anything but...

Reach down and squeeze her ass through her very, very short shorts.

Though I suppose every man has his weaknesses.

Mine is, apparently, my trigger discipline.

The shot streaks through the broken window and embeds itself into his forehead.

Shit.

Carmen is crouched in the corner, and Ivan is dealing with tech-bro number three. The only person to see is...

Mia slams the hilt of her knife into the dead man's forehead, effectively covering the cause of death, before letting him slump to the floor.

She spins on the spot. Turns to look toward the broken window. Her jaw is set and downright furious as she glares.

I'm not even sure if she can see me, but I know from that look that she knows exactly who pulled the trigger.

Before she can do anything else, her attention is snatched by Carmen and she goes running to her side. Gathering the woman up in her arms and hoisting her trembling figure over her shoulder.

Ivan is with them a second later, having dispatched the rest of the men. I can't make out the flurry of words he seems to be yelling at Mia, so I draw back.

The house was by no means empty, and now people are running out the back and spilling onto the front yard in various states of distress.

It won't be long now until the cops arrive.

Ivan shoves Mia and Carmen through the door, and I take the opportunity to pack up my things and make a swift exit of my own.

13

MIA

"I'm so sorry, I'm so sorry," Carmen says for perhaps the hundredth time as I walk her to her front door.

"It's okay, really," I say once again, knowing my reassurance really isn't going to do much. It hasn't so far. "This is what you hired me for."

"I shouldn't have slapped him," she whispers. Big brown eyes staring up at me. She only just stopped crying a few minutes ago.

"If you hadn't, I would've. I'm kinda proud of you, actually."

She half smiles at this. I take it as a win.

"Take it easy, all right?" I back away from the door and head back to the car.

She offers me a wave as I pull away, and I'm suddenly struck by how small she is. Logically, I know she's probably slightly taller than me. But this poor girl seems so unprepared for the world she's been thrust into, and it makes my heart ache a bit.

I focus on that as I drive back to the townhouse, as well as the throbbing pain in my arm that is concealed beneath my jacket. It's easier than thinking about what I'm about to face.

There is probably still glass in the wound. The window had exploded out of nowhere, and I'd shielded Carmen instinctively.

But I wasn't about to pull over to patch it up. Not when the keen sting was the only thing reminding me to keep to the speed limit.

Going home crosses my mind. It would serve him right if I never showed up at the brownstone again.

I tell myself it's my anger that tethers me to him. That the reason I pull up to the familiar building is because confrontation is always inevitable when I'm in this state. I've never shied away from this before; hiding away wouldn't serve me now.

I tell myself it's anger when I open the door and find him waiting at the bottom of the staircase, head in his hands. Dark blonde hair, entirely unkempt, falling over his chocolate eyes.

It has to be the anger. That's the only reason my heart begins to race.

His head snaps up the second I walk in the door.

And oh, oh...the concern in his eyes would make a lesser woman swoon.

But there would be no need for his concern if he hadn't intervened like that.

I wrestle off my jacket and kick off my boots and don't bother lowering my voice. "You weren't supposed to fucking be there."

"You're bleeding."

His words catch me off guard, so I flounder a little as he reaches for my arm to examine my wound.

I shove him away. "You were supposed to stay here and monitor everything from afar. That's what we agreed."

"Come into the kitchen. I need to take a look at that."

"What the hell were you thinking?"

"For God's sake, Mia!" he finally snaps, towering over me in a display of assertiveness that I'm sure works very well to intimidate his little underlings. "Yell at me after you've stopped bleeding all over the carpet."

He pulls firmly at my good arm and half drags me under the overhead light at the kitchen counter.

I try to ignore the fact that this is the first time he's touched me in over a week. But his fingers bear the same calluses that clung to my skin in the throes of ecstasy, and it's so, so hard to concentrate when it feels like he's burning my wrist with his touch.

He disappears for a moment before coming back with a medical kit. I almost laugh at the sight of it: it's huge and definitely war-zone grade, judging by the myriad of thick, slash-proof pouches inside of it.

We had the same one growing up.

"When did this happen?" he asks as he leans over my arm to inspect the damage.

I try not to hiss as he tugs gently at the tender skin. Under the harsh lighting, the long gash seems much deeper than I'd originally thought.

"Window," I grit out. "I think the adrenaline masked the pain."

"There still glass in it?"

I shrug as he pulls out a pair of tweezers and gets to

work. The bleeding has begun to stem, but if I were being totally honest, I would tell him that I need stitches.

"Fuck," I hiss as he applies a little too much pressure extracting a chip of glass.

Wordlessly, he withdraws and comes back with a bottle of whiskey and two glasses before returning to my arm again.

I don't bother with the glasses. I drink right from the bottle.

"I can't believe you drove all the way back like this," he mutters after a moment of silence.

"I can't believe you shot that guy in the head."

He narrows his eyes at me. "I will take you to a hospital," he says it like it's a threat.

"I will bleed all over your carpet," I also say as a threat.

"Are you sure you're mentally sound? You just keep mimicking me. You're usually more original than that."

I scoff as I take another swig of whiskey. "Are you sure you're mentally sound? You—oh fuck!"

It takes everything within me not to jerk my arm away as the pain shoots up my arm with lightning efficiency and shattering agony.

My head must have slumped at one point as I find myself staring at the counter. A hand is soothingly stroking the back of my neck.

"Hey." His voice is so much softer, so much more earnest. Like the last conversation never even existed. "That's it, that's the last of the glass. I'm sorry. I'm sorry."

I squeeze my eyes shut and focus on breathing.

I'm inexplicably comforted by his tone, by the pressure on my neck.

"I've got some skin glue here. It might sting a little when I put it on, but that's it. Okay?"

I nod my head and shudder slightly as he lets me go to tend to my arm again.

There's nothing to be said as he continues to work, fingers diligent and surprisingly gentle. He murmurs a few times to instruct me to move, but the silence that stretches between us has lost the angry charge it had when I arrived.

Something else creeps into this moment, something I don't recognize until Leon has finished wrapping the gauze around my arm and finally decides to voice it.

"I missed you," he sighs so quietly. "Isn't that insane?"

Oh God, I missed him too. A week of nothing, and it was infuriating and awful. And I hated not being able to be here and hated the part of me that wanted to be here. We're a mess.

Instead, I say, "You're the one who walked away."

"You don't want this," he says, but *this* sounds a lot like *me* to my ears.

"I don't," I reply because he said *this* and not *me*. "You don't want me either."

His smirk pierces my heart out of nowhere. It's bitter and doesn't reach his eyes, but it does something very, very warm to my insides.

"That's not what I said."

The warmness crackles from within me, and I'm suddenly very aware that he's still holding my bandaged arm, that we're so close, leaning across the counter.

I swallow hard and fall back on my anger. "Why did you shoot him? I had everything under control, Leon. You could have jeopardized the whole thing."

"He touched you."

"What do you..." the words die in my throat.

Leon looks at me with an intensity that suddenly forces the scattered jigsaw pieces of this entire ordeal into place.

He was *jealous*.

He killed a man because he touched me.

He...

My heart hitches as I stand, walking around the counter toward him, searching his face for confirmation of my theory.

His eyes widen as I approach, backing up against the counter as I crowd him. I take a purposeful step between his legs and watch as he stiffens while his scent overwhelms my senses. How dare he smell so good?

For a beat, we just stand there. Then his eyes drop to my lips, and I just know.

"No one else can have me, can they?" I whisper. "You can't want me, but no one else is allowed, is that it?"

His voice matches mine. "You can do whatever you want. But I will not share you. We've been over this."

"He wasn't..." I pause. There's no anger anymore, no excuse for the way I feel tethered to him now.

He walked away. He didn't want me. I spent all week thinking he didn't want me, but right now? God. "I need to see something."

He swallows as I lean in.

The kiss is chaste, my breath caught in my chest, not quite feeling anything beyond my numb lips. I pull back almost immediately, searching his face for something I swore I saw a moment before.

But his face is entirely blank. Emotionless.

I miscalculated.

I pull away even more. "Shit, I—"

Suddenly, lips crash against mine with such ferocity I'd have stumbled to the floor if it weren't for the arm tightly encircling my back, holding me against his chest.

I'm uncaged, unrestrained, my mouth open and fully claimed. Leon barely lets me breathe, but I don't think I want to anyway.

Because he might have missed me, but I've missed *this*.

I'm losing myself to his touches, drinking him in like a woman parched, and he's just giving and giving and giving.

My good arm wraps around his neck, pulling him in closer and closer, and God, I'm so mad at him. But God do I *need* him.

"I'm not..." I want to swallow the protest, but I need to know. "I'm not ovulating."

"Get rid of those fucking shorts," he hisses, ignoring me entirely as I bite down on his bottom lip. "I never want to see them again."

I take that as an instruction to be fulfilled immediately, judging by the way his hand slips down to my waist.

I pull away to wriggle out of the offending shorts, vaguely aware that things are clattering to the floor around me. I don't have time to check what fell on the ground before his arms are around me again and he's *lifting* me.

I fall into him and take the opportunity to capture his lips again as he sets me on top of the counter. I'm luxuriating in every groan that escapes him as desire begins to pound between my thighs.

He steps between my legs, both hands cradling my face, as he pulls us apart, only to begin worshiping my neck with his mouth and tongue.

"That feels so fucking good," I moan as his teeth begin to tug at the sensitive skin. Marking me, claiming me.

A hand drops between my thighs and palms at the wetness there beneath my panties. It feels like my entire body is on fire. The sounds I make are barely even *human.*

"They can't touch you. They can't look at you. They need to know. They need to know." His growls are like a mantra against my neck, the low timbre of his voice doing nothing but aggravate my already overwhelming desire.

His fingers slip beneath the fabric of my underwear, and I'm like putty in his hands. My good arm is around his neck, hoisting myself up for the perfect angle, turning to find his lips again as I sink onto his hand.

My tightness gives way to his fingers like they were created to be there.

"You're so fucking wet for me," he hisses against my lips. "They can't do this to you, can they? It's me. It's only me."

God. I don't think I can make it upstairs.

I can already feel my juices trickling over his hand as he works me open. His other goes up my shirt, pulling it up so that he can access my chest with his mouth. A tongue slips beneath the fabric of my bra. Teeth nip at the tautness of my nipple.

Something entirely unholy takes over my body.

"There's no one else. No one else has ever—"

"Say you're mine."

"I'm yours." It comes out in a half-scream. "God, fuck me, *please.* I'm yours."

His hands withdraw, then bury themselves in the flesh of my hips. He flips me over on the counter.

Cool granite presses into my cheek, offering me a

moment of clarity as I listen to him taking off his pants. I want this. Goddammit, do I *need this*.

My panties are removed with a tight snap, and then he's there.

Hard, throbbing, touching, but not entering. Letting me learn the sensation, letting me marvel at how strong his desire is for me.

"Please," I beg. "Take me, claim me. No one else. No one else."

He stops hesitating. He sheaths himself to the hilt, and I see fucking stars. Vaguely, I'm aware of the countertop biting into my hips and the low throb of my injured arm, but the pain only adds to the pleasure.

Especially when his hands curl around my hair and yank, arching me into an angle that allows him to push even further.

And it hits, it hits, it...he...fuck.

My brain short circuits. All I can hear is the pounding of his body, slamming into me, over and over.

All I can feel is ecstasy. I don't know if I've already hit my orgasm. I don't know if I'm still riding it out or if it is to come. It's just pure *feeling,* pure rhythm and carnage and craving.

I never want it to end. I want to be used like this forever. I want to drown in the feeling of him inside of me. I want to be resurrected by the hands that grip me tight enough to bruise.

A lifetime passes. An arm scoops me up. His rhythm accelerates. I've come undone at some point. I'm just his to have and to hold.

There's a groan, and I'm lifted up entirely. His lips are on my neck, on the side of my face, desperate and wanting, and *God* do I want them.

He shudders beneath me, and he holds me so, so close as he finishes. His lips are wherever he can find skin, and I sink into his embrace.

Take me, hold me, I'm yours.

And I can't think of any reason at all why that could be a terrible, awful idea.

14

LEON

Mia Natali is a very dangerous and precious thing. It might not be the first time I've thought it, but she surely embodies it in this very moment, lying peacefully in my bed.

In sleep, there's something wholly innocent about her. No frown lines to mar her smooth skin, no flames behind her endlessly green eyes. The effect is entirely angelic.

I'm staring at her when her eyes eventually flutter open, and...no, *now* she looks angelic.

"Good morning." There's a small smile playing in the corner of her mouth.

I lean in to kiss her softly. Her perfect lips are slow to respond and the kiss is chaste, but they send something entirely lovely through my chest.

She sighs into it.

Everything feels easier in the warm morning light, wrapped in sheets, wrapped up in *her*.

"Leon...what is this?"

Even that question feels somehow easier. There's less heat, less anger, less longing.

Her hand reaches for mine. The edge of her bandages crumple slightly as she strokes across my palm.

"I don't know," I confess back. Then, after thinking about it, I say, "Something important."

She nods as if this is a satisfying answer.

We just lay in silence, stealing this moment by stretching it out as long as we can.

"I'm so angry at you. All the time, I'm angry, but there's also *this*." She stops stroking my hand to squeeze it instead. "And then there's *you* who keeps walking away."

I shake my head. "I don't want to, but you didn't choose this. You didn't choose me. You feel obligated, and I can't...I won't take advantage of that."

Her face crumples into something so far from satisfaction she almost looks like an entirely different person. She's still so lovely. She's still lovely when she rolls away onto her back.

"Why did you do it?"

I frown at the question. "Do what?"

"Threaten my father?"

It takes me a second to place a conversation that feels like a lifetime ago. A conversation in an elevator in a hotel with a woman who had just become my wife.

"Mia...I never threatened Marco."

She glances over at me, eyes shining with something distraught. "Don't do that. Don't lie to me."

"I told you I would never do that. I didn't *need* to do that, why would I..." something suddenly clicked. "You never believed me, did you?"

"Just tell me the truth! If you just admit it, then maybe I can…maybe we can talk about it, maybe we can fix this."

A part of me feels a pang of something warm at the thought of forgiveness—only this is not something I need forgiveness for.

"I never threatened him, Mia. I swear it. And…" I take a breath, knowing my next words might just incriminate me further. "I don't think Teo would have either."

"He didn't," she replies with certainty.

Ah. She's spoken to him. She believed him. Which means all this time…

"Look, I think this is something you need to discuss with your father," I say, surprised by how pragmatic the words come out. "But I need you to know that I would never. I could never intentionally hurt you."

Her eyes flicker over to mine, and I pray that she sees the truth in my face.

This has been hurting her. *I've* been hurting her.

"Okay."

My heart skips. "Okay?"

"I'll talk to him."

I let out a breath. "Okay."

The moment stretches again until Mia sighs and gets up.

"I'm sorry," she pauses but continues before I can ask what for. "I didn't get much information for you yesterday. Things went south a lot sooner than expected."

I close my eyes for a moment to realign myself.

"We know that intercepting their shipments has caused them a fair bit of inconvenience. Hopefully, Amos is too distracted trying to placate his clients to notice us working against him."

"Ivan is suspicious of me," Mia says as she pads across the room to grab a bathrobe.

I click my tongue. "I tagged his car before I left. Do you think he'd jeopardize your position with Carmen?"

She turns to look at me, contemplating something with her teeth against her bottom lip. "He told me if I stepped out of line, he'd…" she swallows, "bleed me out in front of those tech guys and let them have me."

Something very cold and very lethal comes over me.

"I think Ivan has outlived his usefulness."

THE TRACKER TAKES us to a factory near the Coney Island Yard, and sure enough, as Max and I pull up a block away, Ivan's sleek, gray Mercedes is parked right outside.

We settle in to wait as long as we need to.

The sky turns slowly gray, and by the time Max is done getting me up to speed on his last meeting with Dante—the Guild is sending the Cartel's stolen merchandise to California—the heavens have opened.

I watch as the rain trickles down the window. It makes it more difficult to see the entrance to the factory, but not impossible.

"Can I ask you something without you biting my head off?" Max says after a pause of comfortable silence.

"That's not a good way to start a conversation." My tone definitely indicates that heads may be bitten off anyhow, but Max continues regardless.

"Why did you swap out with me the other night?"

He's talking about the infiltration at the beach house. I

wrack my brain for a valid excuse. "It was a simple job, no need for both of us to waste our time on it."

"So it had nothing to do with the mercenary?" he asks innocently.

I turn to see my second blinking his eyes at me, a smug little smile slapped on his face. If he wasn't so goddamn useful, I might have wrung his neck then and there.

"You've been talking to Dante."

"Nope," he says, putting emphasis on the "p". "I'm just observant. I wasn't sure if I was right until just now, though."

"Asshole."

"So is it like a thing then?" he presses. "I mean, I get it, she's—"

I cut him off. "She's my wife."

His mouth forms a perfect "O" shape, and he is suddenly looking very sheepish indeed.

"You may as well know," I sigh out. "But we're keeping things...discreet for now."

"Roger that," Max straightens and nods toward the factory doors. "Heads up."

Eyes to the front, we both squint through the rain as a figure spills out. He's hunched and muttering into his phone, and his hand is in his pocket—probably gripping his weapon.

Max shifts beside me, suddenly poised. "He's packing," he murmurs.

Silently, we both exit the car, the hammering rain covering the sound of our movements. The shadows swallow us as we close the distance, boots silent on the rain-slick concrete.

He approaches his car, and his back turns to us. We might be able to subdue him without complications.

Then it happens—his head snaps up, his hand flying from his pocket, the dull gleam of a gun catching the streetlight.

He doesn't hesitate. Neither do I.

The first shot cracks through the night. I pivot, almost imagining that I can feel the rush of air as the bullet grazes past me. My own gun is already in my hand, and its weight is as natural as breathing.

I fire once.

Ivan dives behind his car, swearing violently and scrambling for cover. Max flanks left, his weapon barking twice, warning him that he's outnumbered.

Max and I have him pinned. He's boxed in like an animal.

"How about you come out here and have a little chat with us, Ivan."

Ivan doesn't reply. He knows he's trapped. Max moves silently to the back of the car, waiting for my signal. I see the desperation in Ivan's movements, hear it in the ragged breaths he thinks the rain conceals.

I fire again, the shot deliberate. It ricochets off the hood of the car, inches from his head.

"I don't have all day," I say, my voice cold, lethal. "Come out and face me, you bastard."

Suddenly, Ivan bolts—his last, desperate gamble. He barrels toward the factory, his gun swinging wildly.

"Max," I bark.

Max moves like lightning, slamming into Ivan before he can get far. The two crash to the ground, a tangle of limbs and curses. Before Ivan can recover, I'm there, kicking his weapon out of reach and dragging him up by his collar.

Blood streaks his face, his eyes wide with fear now.

Good. He should be afraid.

"That wasn't so hard, was it?" I say, slamming him against the factory wall. "Now, let's talk a bit about debutantes and tech bros, shall we?"

"I don't know what—" he chokes, trying to find his bravado, but it's gone, "what the fuck you're talking about."

"Bit heartless of Rubio, isn't it? Shoving his only daughter out into the field without any proper training. I wonder what he was thinking."

Something akin to recognition seems to flood his expression. "I knew that fucking ginger—"

My fist connects with his jaw, a sickening crack echoing through the rain.

He crumples to the ground, gasping, bleeding. I crouch, gripping his chin and forcing him to look at me.

"You don't talk about her. You don't think about her," I hiss.

"I'm...n-not tellin' you a thing."

I laugh at this. "Oh, I don't need information from you. That's not what this is. It was your biggest mistake, threatening her, you know? I might have let you live otherwise."

His pupils dilate in realization only a millisecond before I plunge my knife between his ribs.

I lean into his ear as blood begins to gurgle in his mouth. "When I send Amos Rubio to hell after you, tell him it was because he fucked with my family."

15

MIA

I chose a cafe to meet my father. Somewhere neutral where we wouldn't be recognized. Somewhere away from the prying eyes of the Guild or the Prince's Hand or, I suppose, the Cartel now.

Not that I think anyone has any reason to be interested in me just yet, but I can't bring myself to show up on his doorstep, and my apartment is too small for two.

I've not really seen Marco since the wedding, not since he dropped off the wedding gift that I still haven't worn or sold yet. He'd been treading on eggshells that day, which I'd chalked up to the absurdity of the situation.

Now, as he enters the store and I watch him tell the barista his order, I can still see that same tension in his shoulders.

And when he sits next to me, there's guilt in his eyes. Or is it shame? Or is it the weight of knowing his life choices resulted in marrying his daughter off to a don?

"*Papà,*" I greet him with a kiss on either cheek.

His fingers linger on my bandaged arm as I pull away.

"You're hurt," his voice catches slightly. "He said he wouldn't hurt you."

"I hurt myself," I say firmly, suddenly feeling oddly protective of his opinion of Leon. "Hazards of the job."

Marco grits his teeth. "What job?"

I give him a pointed look. "Well, I'm not working at the *Candelabra* anymore."

"You swore you would leave that life behind." He's gripping my hand now, a little desperately. The pressure of his grip sends a dull pain up my arm. "You're a wife now, soon to be a mother. He shouldn't be allowing you to keep playing these games."

Something akin to dread begins to pool in my stomach. "Allowing me?"

"I only agreed to this because he said he would keep you *safe*."

I feel a bubble of laughter in my throat. "You wanted me to be safe? You shouldn't have married me off to a mafia don."

"It was safer than anything Teo suggested," he says as if that is a valid reason. "He would have had you as the face of his new business venture. At least Leon promised to keep you a secret."

The coffee in front of me is burning hot. I wrap my fingers around the porcelain anyway, pressing them in tight.

"I'm only going to ask you this one time," I say softly. "So I'm going to need you to be honest with me. I deserve that much, don't I?"

My father lets out a long breath and nods firmly, staring at a spot just over my shoulder.

"Who threatened your life?"

He blanches. "What?"

"You said that you'd die if I didn't go through with the wedding. Who made that threat?"

"Mia—"

"Because it wasn't Teo." I can hear my voice raising slightly. "And Leon claims he didn't do it either. I'll admit I was hesitant to trust him on that, but you haven't looked me in the eye since you sat down."

He cringes slightly as he forces his eyes to mine. "Please, Mia. You need to understand…"

"What? That my own father was the one manipulating me this whole time?" I shoot the accusation out and send up a silent prayer that he'll deny it.

Marco Chiavari swallows.

"It's getting very, very dangerous out there."

I stand up, the scrape of my chair a brutal, deafening sound against our hushed conversation. "You *lied* to me."

"I didn't lie," he insists, reaching for my arm.

I snatch it away. "You manipulated me."

"You are the only thing that matters to me, Mia. The *only* thing." He stands too. "It would kill me if anything happened to you. I wouldn't be able to live with myself, do you understand that?"

Vaguely, I'm aware that our discussion is starting to garner some attention.

"It's my fault you're in this life…mine. That's on me until my dying breath. I would do anything to go back and change it," he says, his voice breaking slightly at the end. "You're my little girl. This is the best I could do for you, and I *know* it will never be enough."

I can feel tears prickling in my eyes as I take a step back, away from him. This is the man I have always trusted. "You're right. It's not enough."

"Mia. Please, honey." He crumbles a bit as he tries to follow me.

But I shake him off. "I need you to leave me alone for a bit, okay? No more meddling. No more gifts, no more trying to pay my rent. I don't need it. I never needed it. You can just leave me alone."

"I'm your father—"

"You never *trusted* that I'd be able to handle myself. Never. I build a life for myself on the back of my own skill and my own strengths and my own work, and you think you have the right to just fly in and...and...wave a wand and put me in a safe little box away from *everything* I ever loved."

I swallow hard and look him dead in the eyes. "Fuck you, Dad."

The bass thrums in the air before we even reach the club's entrance, a deep, pulsing heartbeat that seems to shake the pavement under my heels.

Neon lights flicker above the doorway, casting the word "Inferno" in blood-red letters against the slick black sky. The line stretches halfway down the block, a sea of people eager to drown their troubles in music and tequila.

"Are you sure about this?" I glance sideways at Carmen, who's practically vibrating with excitement.

Her dark curls tumble over her shoulders and her red dress clings to her like a second skin. She looks every bit the confident cartel princess she is, but there's a softness in her smile that's pure Carmen.

"Absolutely," she says, looping her arm through mine. It feels so oddly familiar now. "I needed to thank you for the catastrophe that was the beach house, and you look tense as shit. It's a win, win."

It had been slightly strange to receive her call a week ago. At first, I thought she wanted me on another job, but as it transpired, she'd just wanted to talk.

It started with her just trying to process what had happened at the beach house. But then she started to complain about Ivan, which turned into worrying that Ivan had gone missing. Then, inexplicably, she was asking me about school and my goals, and my life.

In the boring monotony that had become my life, Carmen had become something of a highlight.

Especially as Leon hadn't been back to the brownstone all week. Not that I'd been checking (I had). I hadn't really confronted him about anything after the blowout with my father.

He's been busy ever since Ivan "went missing", and I've honestly appreciated the space.

Somehow, this week of distance felt easier than the last. I think knowing that there would be a conversation at the end of it made it easier.

One where I apologize for thinking the worst of him.

One where, maybe, we can start to fix something that shouldn't have been so broken in the first place.

It feels like something…important. Something to take our time over. And I can't deny having a week to get my thoughts together has done wonders for my general anxiety over the entire situation.

"Fine, but if you get into trouble, I'm hauling your ass out of here," I jest back.

As we approach the bouncer, Carmen barely spares him

a glance. He steps aside immediately, lifting the velvet rope with a nod—the perks of her last name.

Inside, the club is pure, glorious chaos. The music is deafening, a thundering beat that reverberates through my chest.

Colored lights slice through the darkness, flashing across a packed dance floor where bodies move in a hypnotic rhythm. The air smells of sweat, alcohol, and just a hint of danger.

Carmen drags me straight to the bar, leaning in to shout her order to the bartender. "Two shots of tequila and two margaritas!"

"Carmen—"

"No arguments!" She grins, pressing a shot glass into my hand. "We're celebrating."

I raise an eyebrow. "Celebrating what?"

"Us. Surviving. That we're still breathing." She clinks her glass against mine. "That's enough, don't you think?"

I don't argue. I pretend to down the shot in one go, wincing as if the burn is setting a fire in my chest when in reality, I dumped the liquid on the floor. Carmen is too preoccupied with her own shot to notice.

For the next few hours, we lose ourselves in the wonderful chaos.

Carmen is a natural on the dance floor, her movements fluid and carefree. She twirls, pulling me into her orbit, and for a little while, the tension in my shoulders eases.

I stay close, scanning the crowd out of habit, but I let myself relax enough to enjoy the moment and the buzz of bodies around me and the beating of a collective heartbeat through the speakers.

I'd told Leon I'd be here, just in case. It felt like the smart thing to do, and he'd texted me to be careful. Which was fine, honestly. It was very cool of him, very reserved, very mature after his response the last time I went out with Carmen.

Except there's a part of me that really does want him to be here this time. Maybe it's the press of skin against skin all around me, maybe it's the hypnotic dancing, but I'm looking for chocolate brown in the eyes of every stranger who crosses my path.

By the time we make our way back to the bar, we're both flushed and breathless. Carmen orders another round, her smile wide and genuine.

"See?" she says, leaning against the counter. "This is what we needed!"

I study her, the way her eyes sparkle in the flashing lights, the way her laughter seems to make the world a little brighter. It hits me then how much I've come to care for her.

Not as a client, not as the daughter of my enemy, but as Carmen.

"I think you're good for me, Cammy," I admit, and her grin widens.

"I think you're good for me, too."

The rest of the night blurs into a haze of music, laughter, and stolen moments of peace. For a little while, I forget about the danger, the lies, and the tightrope I'm walking.

Then the music shifts, a sultry beat that pulls the crowd closer together, bodies pressed together, barely a breath apart. A hand slides over my hip, firm but careful, and I stiffen on instinct.

"Easy," a deep voice murmurs in my ear, the sound barely cutting through the music.

It's a voice I know.

Before I can turn, the stranger moves in time with me, his other hand grazing the curve of my waist. The scent hits me next—rum spice and black pepper, warm and achingly familiar.

I freeze, my breath catching in my throat.

Leon.

I whip my head around, meeting the eyes I've been looking for all night beneath the brim of a low-slung cap. It's him. Disguised, hidden in plain sight, but undeniably him.

"What are you doing here?" I hiss, my body still moving in sync with his despite the fact my heart is trying to beat out of my chest.

"Dancing with my wife," he says, his tone casual but edged with heat.

My heart lurches. "You're insane," I snap, even as my body betrays me, pressing closer to his.

"Maybe." His lips curve into a small, dangerous smile, and his hands tighten on my waist, pulling me flush against him. "But I've been watching you all night, and I couldn't stay away."

I glance over my shoulder, searching for Carmen. She's still by the bar, laughing with someone who looks like they're trying too hard.

"You shouldn't be here," I say, my voice lower now, almost pleading. God knows I'm going to lose all motivation to send him away if he keeps touching me like this.

"I know."

I swallow hard, my pulse roaring in my ears. I'm letting him guide me through the song like we're the only two people who can even hear it.

When the song ends, he leans in, his lips brushing my ear. "You look beautiful, by the way."

Then, just as quickly as he appeared, he slips into the crowd, disappearing into the shadows.

I'm left standing there, my body humming with the aftermath of his touch, my mind in complete disarray.

"Mia!" Carmen's voice cuts through the haze, and I turn to see her making her way over, having ditched her admirer, blissfully unaware of the storm raging inside me.

I plaster on a smile and pretend that everything is absolutely, positively fine.

16

LEON

"Permission to speak freely, sir?"

The voice in my ear sounds professional, but there's an undercurrent to the tone that already has me gritting my teeth. "No."

He does so anyway. "You should really work on your two-step."

I make a point of looking over across the room to where Max is lounging by the bar and flash him a middle finger.

"Real subtle there, boss," the voice is now Dante's from somewhere over on the dancefloor.

Teo's second had been in the office when Mia had messaged. I should have realized he'd seemed a little too eager to help out and probably asked a few more questions about his intentions.

For the last few hours, I've had to watch him alternate between dancing with two very attractive women. This wasn't a mission for him; this was his playground, and it was starting to get old.

"Stay in your own damn lane, Grasso," I snap.

Dante presses himself up against yet another blonde. "Gladly."

My eyes absently flick back down to the bar, to where Mia is listening to Carmen explain something with slightly too elaborate hand gestures. The debutant has been drinking solidly for several hours now, so it's no surprise.

Mia has a lovely flush to her cheeks, one that I know isn't the result of alcohol—considering that she's been subbing out every drink Carmen puts in front of her with water.

It's been a very long week. That's the excuse I give myself. The possibility that I'm the reason behind that flush is enough to make me half-hard.

Fuck, I was ready to take her right then on the dancefloor.

I need to get myself together.

Mia gets up from her seat and pointedly doesn't look around before beelining to the bathroom. Maybe I could...

"I'll follow her," Max announces. I see the man already shifting from his seat.

Good. That's good. That's a sensible thing to do. This is still, technically, work.

Fucking my wife in a bathroom wouldn't be very professional.

I sit back in my seat and try my best to focus on the job. Just another couple of hours, then I can make up some kind of excuse to see her again. Maybe she'll come back to the brownstone with me.

Maybe she'll explain then why her father hasn't shown up to work all week.

My phone rings, and I frown down at the caller ID. It's almost three a.m. He never calls this late.

"Teo?"

"Where are you?" The Guild's don barks down the phone. "The Cartel is mobilizing for fucking battle in the middle of the goddamn night. I need everyone you can spare."

All thoughts of warmth and thighs and a bathroom rendezvous entirely leave my mind. "Where? One of ours?"

"Brooklyn, but neutral. No one's stationed there, but they're launching an attack on someone…"

"…and an enemy of an enemy is a friend," I finish for him. "What's the address?"

"The Inferno, it's a club on Liberty. Cars have been swarming it for twenty minutes."

No.

I stand up and immediately look toward the bathroom, where both Max and Mia have disappeared from view.

No. No. No.

"Leon?"

My voice feels dead in my throat. "I'm already here."

The lights cut out.

The club plunges into darkness, the air vibrating with the pulse of the bass and the sudden cries of the crowd. Panicked or excited, it's suddenly very hard to tell.

The only source of light comes from the sickly green strobes that scatter across the crowds too frequently to be of any use. This is bad.

"Did you just say you're already at The Inferno?" Teo's voice crackles over the phone.

"Yeah. In the middle of this fucking mess," I growl, my hand going for my gun. "I'm going to need you guys at every exit pushing in. Expect heavy foot traffic. Dante is already on the floor. I'll get him to link up comms with you. How many—"

"Too many for the two of you, heavily armed."

"Max is here too, somewhere. So is..." I swallow hard. "So is Mia."

There's a pause before Teo answers, his tone grim. "Shit. Do you think they're after her?"

Gunfire erupts near the DJ booth. Strobe lights flash, casting broken glimpses of chaos: terrified faces, bodies surging toward exits, and shadows moving with purpose through the confusion.

"We're out of time. You need to move in now," I bark, already making my way toward the floor, toward the last place I saw her. My feet move of their own accord like she's a magnet that I'm drawn to.

I have to find her.

"We'll get her out," Teo says as if sensing my thoughts. "Watch your back."

The line goes dead as I shove my way through the panicked crowd, scanning the room through the shifting darkness for any sign of her.

Max went after her. He'd keep her safe, wouldn't he? He'd make sure she got out.

But my instincts are too busy screaming that something's wrong for this to be much consolation.

Something slams into my shoulder, and I turn on impact—noting the dark clothes of my assailant and the way his eyes glimmer in recognition as he looks at me. I have a split second to register his intent before his fist starts its trajectory toward my face.

My forearm is up to block in an instant, sweeping out with my leg while his momentum is carrying him forward. His legs buckle, and he falls unceremoniously to the floor, soon to be lost to the stampede of patrons rushing past.

I manage to yank hold of his collar and retaliate with a blow of my own. Once, twice. I hit him three times in the face, then draw him up to bark in his ear over the noise, ignoring the way the blood trickling from his nose smears across my cheek.

"What are you doing here?"

His response is to claw at my arm, to start struggling to free himself. Then, with one sharp movement, he turns his face to the side and ferally bites down on my ear.

The pain jolts through me as I wrench him away. It's pure instinct to reach for his neck, the snapping noise lost in the sea of sound that erupts once more as a spray of gunfire flashes above our heads.

"Leon!" Dante's voice cuts through the noise, and I turn to see him sprinting toward me, blood streaking his temple. "Max is down—found him near the bathrooms, unconscious but alive."

The words hit me like a punch to the gut. "Mia?"

Dante shakes his head, his expression grim.

Don't think about it. She's fine. She's fine. She has to be fine.

"Teo is outside. Set up a comms link. He should have the Guild ready to intercept by now," I shout over another scream. The gunfire is getting closer.

"What about you?"

"I need to find Mia."

"Leon—"

But I've already started running. "Go. Now. That's an order."

Progress is slower now as I push and push and push against the current of people desperately trying to reach the exits. Flashes of faces are illuminated by the sickly green strobe lights and the erratic gunfire.

A shot goes off too close for comfort, and I drop with those around me immediately in self-preservation. The sudden space gives me a clear line of sight across the room.

A looming figure, a close-shaved head, and a leather jacket. Gesturing and barking orders at men dressed head to toe in black. They all look just like the man I incapacitated before.

Only I know this stance, know the grim line of that expression. Even in the dim light, his presence is unmistakable.

Amos Rubio.

In the flesh. In the middle of The Inferno.

The man who hasn't been seen outside his precious mansion in months is now barking orders to the Cartel in the middle of a populated venue.

This is very, very bad.

I flick off the safety on my gun as I change course toward him. But my line of sight gets disrupted as the bodies around me begin to move again.

Some civilian with a hero complex sees my gun and tries to wrestle me for it. It's easy to knock him aside, but the momentary distraction costs me. I lose sight of Rubio completely.

I spin around, trying to relocate the place he'd been only a moment earlier, to no avail. My movements become more agitated and desperate until...

Something cold and hard presses into the back of my neck.

"Leon Moretti," he drawls, overwhelmingly arrogant. "Why am I not surprised that you're here?"

My entire body tenses as Amos Rubio strolls casually into view. His grip on his gun is lazy as he circles around me.

"Teo Vitale has you doing his dirty work. I'd hoped you'd have more of a backbone, but then again, the Guild has always had a way of chewing people up and spitting them back out again."

He steps closer, tilting his head. "You chose the wrong side, Moretti. I could have given you so much more than this."

It's all just games, trying to buy time or distract me.

"Where is she?" I demand, my voice low and dangerous.

"Who?" he asks, feigning innocence. "Teo's little spy? Or my precious daughter?"

My stomach hollows out. He knows. He knows about Mia.

Do you think they're after her?

"It's my fault, really. I underestimated Teo. Using my darling, naive Carmen like that, luring her out to a place like this in order to what, kidnap her? Torture her for information?" Amos sucks at his teeth.

Wait. Does he think we're here for *Carmen?*

"Not really his style. But then I realized," Amos taps his gun to my chin. "It's your style, isn't it? Leon Natali, the man who killed his own mother in cold blood. The man who would send his wife into the field to manipulate a child."

My mind goes blank. A faint buzzing fills my ears. He can't know about that. How does he know about that?

It must register on my face because his face splits into a cruel smile. "You were careless, Leon, killing Ivan like that. We were on to your precious Mia before, but you were the one that made us really look. Why else would the don of the Prince's Guild dispatch Ivan personally?"

He leans in closer. "What was it you said? 'Tell Amos Rubio this is because you fucked with my family'?"

He'd heard everything. Probably had cameras all over that damn building, and I'd just waltzed in without thinking.

This is all my fault. Mia is in danger because of *me*.

I need to get out of this. I need backup. My eyes dart around us. The crowd is beginning to thin. But there are too many men in black surrounding us now, monitoring the conversation.

Teo will be here soon. I just need a bit more time.

"Where is Mia?"

The man chuckles and pulls away. "You know, I don't think I'm going to tell you that. I want you to panic the way I did when I learned that you'd lured Carmen out here."

"Carmen came here herself." Something darts through my peripheral vision, and I do my best to keep staring at the man before me.

Amos shakes his head. "Carmen is a good girl. She knows what's expected of her. She would never come to a place like this where she could be...so easily tarnished."

Before I have time to grimace, there's an almighty crash, and suddenly, men are bursting into the room from all sides.

Amos' temporary distraction is the opening I need to smack his arm up. His gun goes off—as if he instinctively pulled the trigger—and the bullet narrowly misses me as it blasts into the air.

I pull back to lift up my own gun, but Amos is already there, faster than I could have anticipated. He slams down on my arm, making me drop it, and I narrowly manage to dodge a second attack by throwing myself to the floor.

Amos is on me before I can fully recover, his weight slamming into me like a freight train. I helplessly watch my gun skitter across the ground as we crash into each other, blow meeting blow as I try to get back on my feet.

He's strong, his fists relentless as he drives me to defend over and over. But I'm faster.

I twist, using his momentum against him, and land a hard punch to his ribs. He grunts, stumbling back, but recovers quickly. His knife flashes in the dim light, and I barely dodge the blade, feeling the rush of air as it slices past my cheek.

I catch his wrist, twisting until the knife drops from his grasp, and slam him against the floor.

"Where is she?" I snarl, my forearm pressed against his throat.

Amos laughs, blood staining his teeth. "You're too late, Moretti. She's already mine."

17

MIA

Getting ambushed in a bathroom stall hadn't really been on my agenda for the day. Serves me right for thinking that a woman's bathroom in a club was some kind of sacred space.

I let my guard down for thirty seconds, and now I'm being half-wrestled, half-dragged out of the room and into the chaos of the dance floor.

My heels skid against the sticky floor as I thrash, but my captor's grip is ironclad.

"Let go of me!" I shout, clawing at the stranger's arm.

He doesn't answer, his face shadowed by the erratic strobe lights.

It's hard to get a read on him; there's nothing about their dark clothes that identifies their affiliation, but I'm not an idiot, either. I don't have many enemies that would accost me in a bathroom.

And if the Cartel are here...

... does that mean Carmen set me up?

The potential betrayal stings with bitter irony, and I try

not to dwell on it. I'd betrayed her first, right? I had this coming.

But we'd been laughing together only moments ago. Had she known then? Was this whole night—the first night I'd actually enjoyed in so long—just one big manipulation? Was any of it real?

I wasn't supposed to care for my client, but Carmen had molded herself so easily into the cracks of my heart.

I grit my teeth as my assailant's grip tightens, jerking me toward a side exit as the crowd surges in the opposite direction.

I catch flashes of movement—a woman screaming, a man shoving past with wild eyes—but no one seems to notice me being hauled away.

My captor's pace quickens, and I twist, desperate for any opening. Then I see him.

Leon.

My eyes lock on him, and my heart clenches. Leon is a whirlwind of motion, grappling with Amos Rubio on the floor. The Cartel kingpin is fighting like a cornered animal, vicious and unrelenting, but Leon is just about holding his own.

But others are closing in on them too, men in black who have yet to be intercepted by...fuck, is that the *Guild*? When did they get here?

"Stop struggling," my attacker growls as I attempt to yank myself free again. My eyes are still trained on Leon, refusing to lose him in the chaos of the crowd.

Fights are breaking out all around, but no one from our side seems to have spotted the two dons rolling about on the floor.

The fight is too evenly matched. I watch in horror as Rubio's knife slices too close to Leon's throat.

He needs me. Now.

"Get. Your. Hands. Off. Me," I hiss, each word said clearly and with spite. My words are the only warning I give before I use the pressure on my arm to walk myself up his body and wrap my thighs around his neck.

The sudden extra body weight has him toppling to the floor, releasing his grip on me in order to break his fall.

I land on top of him, using his ribs to cushion the blow, before scrambling off into the crowd. Pulling my knife from its sheath, I charge at the figure that has finally managed to find his footing.

Amos Rubio stands tall, knife twirling expertly in his hand as he steps forward toward Leon's prone body.

I don't think, I just launch myself at the kingpin's back and bury my knife in his shoulder.

Rubio hisses in pain and snatches his knife up in his non-dominant hand to try and swipe at me blindly. I drop low to avoid him, only for him to kick me in the chest and send me hurtling to the floor.

"*Mia.*"

Leon is kneeling over in a second, his eyes flashing with both relief and fury.

"Seems like you need a hand," I wheeze, ignoring the pain in my ribs.

Behind us, Amos is wrenching my knife from his shoulder with a cry of anguish.

"You need to get the hell out of here," Leon growls as his arm slips around my waist to pull me to my feet.

A part of me sighs in relief at the feeling of being pulled into his chest. He's solid and alive. So very alive.

But he needs to stay that way, and I can't be sure he will unless I'm here, too. "Are you being serious right now? You almost just got yourself killed!"

"This isn't a discussion!"

My knife flies through the space between us. It would have embedded itself in my cheek had Leon not pushed me back.

"Mia, get out of here!" Leon growls as he goes to meet Amos' swing, ducking under it and slamming a fist into his face.

"Not a chance!" I yell back, dropping low to avoid the wild swing of his blade, trying to disarm him.

Amos leaps back before I can, wiping blood from his mouth. His eyes gleam with rage as he looks between us.

"So, it's true," he sneers, his words dripping with venom. "The little mercenary and the Italian don. How quaint."

"Shut up and fight," I snap.

Amos lunges first, his knife flashing in the strobe lights. I block his strike, twisting his wrist to disarm him, but he counters with another brutal punch to my ribs that sends me staggering.

Leon is on him instantly, as if we'd been training together for years, driving Amos back with a series of precise strikes. Blood spatters on the floor as Leon lands a blow to Amos's jaw, but the Cartel kingpin doesn't go down easily.

I recover quickly, circling around to flank Amos, watching as Leon grabs Amos' injured arm, twisting it behind his back. I step in to try to snatch the knife from his hand once more.

Amos roars in pain as my fingers wrap around the

handle, trying to use the distraction to pry the damn thing away.

It doesn't occur to me that he might be faking.

It doesn't occur to me until the second his grip miraculously tightens, and the knife is suddenly on a trajectory to my chest.

"NO!"

I'm shoved to the floor brutally, gasping at the bruising pain in my side. I spin frantically to where…

…to where Leon has taken a knife to his gut.

"LEON!"

He staggers back, grimacing in pain as Amos towers over him.

"Now you want to play the hero, Natali?" Rubio sneers at him.

I see red. I see flashes of sickly green. I see something glint on the floor, trampled under too many feet but close enough to reach.

Leon tries a weak swing, but Rubio deflects it easily.

"This is what happens to Teo Vitale's lap dogs."

My fingers reach and reach, then close. A familiar weight settles back into my hand.

I launch myself at Amos Rubio. We both go tumbling to the floor as I slam his arm and hand under my knee, sending his knife skittering across the floor. My other knee punches into his gut as he tries to grapple us into a more dominant position.

But I have him pinned. He has no weapon.

And he can't move an inch without my knife skewering his neck.

I raise my knife, ready to finish the job, but a voice freezes me in place.

"Stop!"

I whip around to see Carmen standing a few feet away, her wide eyes locked on the scene before her. Her face is pale, her red dress torn and smeared with blood.

"Carmen," I whisper.

Her gaze shifts from me to Leon, then to her father, pinned and bleeding on the floor. The realization dawns slowly, horror creeping across her features.

"Mia..." Her voice is a broken whisper.

My chest tightens, the knife trembling in my hand. Amos uses the distraction to throw me off with his remaining strength, and I let him, suddenly trapped by the woman's distressed gaze.

"Carmen, it's not what you think," I say, crawling toward her, but she backs away, shaking her head.

"It's exactly what I think," her voice rising. "You've been lying to me this whole time. You're with *him*. You're with the Italians!"

"Cammy, please."

"I *trusted* you!"

The word cuts deeper than I expect, and I falter, guilt crashing over me like a tidal wave.

"Carmen," Amos's voice weakly breaks through the moment. "Get out of here. Now."

But she doesn't move. Instead, her eyes stay locked on mine, betrayal etched into every line of her face.

For one terrible moment, I think she might attack. The thought certainly seems to cross her mind as she takes a purposeful step forward toward me.

I scramble to my feet, whipping my knife around defensively in alarm.

Her eyes widen as she retreats a small step.

Oh.

She hadn't been trying to attack.

But now she knew that I would.

Something shatters in her expression before it goes icy cold. "You're dead to me." Carmen stares at me a moment longer before going to her father's side.

Around us, people are still fighting, screaming, and yelling orders. I turn to Leon, where he's half-propped himself up on the ground. I reach for him, and between us, we manage to get him to his feet.

"We need to go," I say. "Can you walk?"

"Just go," he hisses.

Leon's weight sags heavily against me as I begin to drag him toward the exit. By the time I think of looking back over my shoulder, Carmen and Amos are nowhere to be found.

"I don't think he hit anything important," Leon grunts as we make it out into the fresh hair.

Blood soaks through his shirt, staining my hands as I clutch his side around the still-embedded knife anyway, trying to keep pressure on the wound. I try not to think about how labored his breathing is.

The chaos of the club fades into the background, replaced by the rhythmic pounding of my heart and the echo of Carmen's words.

You're dead to me.

Ahead of us are a group of men hurriedly shoving people into cars and barking orders. Thankfully, they notice us quickly.

"What the hell happened to you two?" Teo shouts.

Dante leans heavily against Teo, his own face pale and streaked with blood. There's another man a few steps behind, clutching his arm where a makeshift bandage is wrapped around his arm.

Leon stirs at my side. "Amos. He thought we were kidnapping Carmen. He had Mia."

"But I got away," I finish for him. "Teo, he needs medical attention."

Before Teo can answer, Leon lets out an indignant, "I'm fine."

The man behind Teo chucks me a set of car keys. "Mia, get him in the car and go."

"Stay out of this, Max," Leon barks.

"With all due respect, no," Max counters firmly. "It's my fault she got caught. Now, both of you need to get out of here."

Leon grunts, trying to push himself upright. "I can fight," he insists, but the tremor in his voice betrays him.

"Shut up," I hiss. "You can barely stand."

"Exactly. You've done enough tonight. We're not discussing this," Teo says with all the authority of a don.

I nod, pulling Leon toward the waiting car before he can attempt another protest. Max helps me get him into the passenger seat, his head lolling back as he lets out a ragged breath. His face is pale, his shirt soaked with crimson.

"You're going to be fine," I say, trying to keep my voice steady as I buckle him in.

"Mia," he murmurs, his hand brushing mine. His touch is weak, but it's enough to make my chest ache.

"Don't talk," I say, blinking back tears as I climb into the driver's seat.

The car roars to life, and I floor the accelerator, tearing out onto the empty street. I keep one hand on the wheel and the other pressed against Leon's side, praying the bleeding will slow.

"Hold on," I whisper, more to myself than to him.

"Mia," he says again, his voice barely audible.

"I said don't talk."

"Carmen," he mutters, and the sound of her name is like a dagger to my chest.

"I know," I choke out, my throat burning with unshed tears. "I know."

The image of her face flashes in my mind—those wide, betrayed eyes, the way her voice broke as she called me a traitor. My hands tighten on the wheel as I fight the urge to scream.

"I ruined everything," I whisper, my voice trembling.

"It wasn't your fault. It was me. I gave you away."

I swallow down the lump in my throat. Now isn't the time. "Shush now, okay? We can talk about it when you don't have a knife in your gut."

"Please..." Leon's voice is terribly faint. I fly through a red light.

"Shush, Leon. Please."

"Stay with me."

The tears spill over.

"Yes. Yes. Anything."

18

LEON

The drive to the city outskirts is a blur, pain radiating from the knife wound in my side with every bump in the road.

Mia sits stiff beside me, her knuckles white as she grips the steering wheel. She barely speaks, her focus sharp, but I catch the way she glances at me every few seconds, her worry etched across her face.

It takes me a moment to realize where we are when we pull to a stop. Mia is moving the second she cuts the ignition, and the older man runs to her aid in an instant.

"You're lucky she got you here when she did," Marco mutters as he presses gauze to the deep gash in my abdomen. "Another inch and that blade would've punctured something vital."

Lucky. I bite back a bitter laugh.

Mia hasn't left the room, not even when Marco snapped at her to stay out of his way. She stood back, arms crossed, her eyes fixed on me the entire time like her focus alone could keep me alive.

When Marco finally stitches me up and straps a makeshift dressing over my side, he turns to her. "He's stable for now, but this isn't a hospital. He needs rest, clean bandages, and someone to keep him from tearing those stitches."

She nods sharply, already moving to help me sit up. I don't miss the way her hand recoils when Marco reaches for her.

"Mia," he says her name like a plea.

"Thank you for saving him," her voice is cool. "I'll take it from here."

The man looks desperately at his daughter for a moment longer before sagging into his chair with his head between his hands.

"Come on," she whispers as she helps me up. Neither of us looks back at the older man as we leave.

The ride back to the brownstone is substantially slower than the last. My body feels like lead, exhaustion dragging me under. Mia says nothing, but I can feel the tension rolling off her, thick and suffocating.

When she pulls up in front of the house, she's out of the car before I can even open the door.

"Let's get you to bed," she says, her voice brisk as she slings my arm over her shoulder and helps me up the steps.

Stairs, as it would turn out, are not a good combination with new stitches, but eventually, I manage to make it to my room, grunting in relief as I lie back on the pillows and close my eyes.

I'm not sure how long I lie there, but when I open my eyes again, Mia is still hovering over the bed. Her beautiful face is pale and battling through a myriad of emotions.

"Mia..."

"I'm sorry," the words burst out of her with alarming volume. "You shouldn't have jumped in front of the knife."

"I wasn't about to let you die," I counter firmly. "You should have left when I told you to."

She shakes her head. "I wasn't about to let you die either."

"Has anyone ever told you how stubborn you are?"

"Has anyone ever told you you're a hypocrite?"

She smiles, and it breaks something within me to watch as this pushes her over the edge. Her hand clamps over her mouth, her shoulders shaking. I want to hold her so desperately. The longing is more painful than the stab wound in my side.

"I'm s-sorry. I'll go."

"No, please." The words feel oddly familiar on my tongue. "Stay with me."

She hesitates a moment, her eyes bright with tears, before turning to switch off the lights. The relief of the feeling of the bed dipping as she slides in beside me is unparalleled.

The darkness offers us something more than a reprieve from the horrors of the day—it's a space where actions feel less consequential. My arm slides around her shoulders, bringing her as close to my body as I can manage.

She must think so, too, as she doesn't protest, gently burying her head into my shoulder.

"I thought I was going to lose you," I confess into the darkness. "When you attacked Rubio, I thought I was going to have to watch you die."

"Leon..." A warm hand rests itself against my cheek.

"I don't think I would survive it."

A thumb brushes against my skin. "Sleep. I promise I'll still be here in the morning."

SHE STAYS. She stays the whole day. Stays the next day, too. At some point, I think she must have left because her clothes changed. When I ask her about it, she tells me she moved a few things into her room.

She doesn't sleep there, though. Every night, she fusses over my wound and lingers by the bed until I utter those same words again.

"Stay with me."

And she turns off the light and slides next to me.

It's both the most glorious experience and the most brutal. To have her so close, yet so unfairly far.

Rationally, I know it's the guilt that makes her stay. I know it's her sense of duty and obligation.

But in the fragile truce between us, it's so, so easy to imagine it could be something more.

She tells me her father confessed to threatening her himself. I hadn't thought Marco would have it in him, but the act had clearly left a painful smear on their relationship.

I don't pry. I don't ask any more than she's willing to share. But there's this traitorous thought that screams *what are you waiting for?*

She lies in my bed every night. I feel her warmth buried in my side. I feel her heartbeat. She's alive and well and her heart is beating and beating. She's safe. It's enough to drive me mad with longing. My self-control champs at the bit as I reign it into submission.

The following week, Teo visits with an update. Of

course, that update is that there *is* no update. Only that the Cartel has made a retreat and that our marriage is now common knowledge.

"You're both likely at the top of their hit list," Teo explains as he leaves. "I suggest you lie low for a while."

I wave him off. It's not as if I can do much else. The wound is healing well, but Mia has been treating me like I've been made of glass, refusing to let me do much more than walk down the corridor and back.

That night, when she frets at my side, I relay the news.

"Good." She bobs her head. "You shouldn't be doing anything but resting anyway."

I roll my eyes at her. "I'm perfectly fine. I've been cleared for physical activity."

"*Light* physical activity," Mia counters.

And God, she looks incredible when she pouts like that, with her arms crossed under her breasts and that adorable wrinkle between her eyebrows as she frowns. It's enough to drive a man mad.

"Then it's a good thing that there are many ways to perform *light* physical activity."

The words escape before I have much time to register what I've said. The flirtatious undertones linger between us as if waiting to drop like a lead balloon.

Mia blinks a couple of times, her mouth dropping into that perfect "O" shape that is far too kissable for its own good. She drops down, perching on the edge of the bed next to me.

"You shouldn't say things like that to me," she replies quietly.

I laugh to try to break the tension. "You're my wife."

"Leon." It's a warning.

I sigh. "I'm sorry. I don't want to make you uncomfortable."

Her green eyes flash to mine in annoyance. "It's not that."

"Then what are you talking about?"

"I'm talking about the fact that if I have to sleep by your side for another night without sucking your cock, I might actually go insane," she half-yells. "And I can't do that because you're still hurt, and I—"

I've already bridged the gap between us. Already reached for her neck to pull her in.

I'm a man entirely possessed as I press her mouth to mine.

And dear fucking God.

I've missed this. I miss it even in those brief moments when my lips aren't pressed to hers in order to take a breath. I wish I could cut out my own lungs and just kiss her forever.

She tastes divine as I lick into her mouth. She opens up for me gorgeously as I explore every inch of it. Our tongues are battling for dominance as she makes a sound so delicious I want to taste every decibel.

Her hands find themselves in my hair, tugging me ever closer. Not close enough. Never close enough. But the feeling of her body pressed into mine makes me feel complete for the first time in weeks.

"We shouldn't," she hisses as my mouth trails down her neck. "We shouldn't do this."

I respond with my teeth, and she squirms delightfully as I suck on the flesh below her ear. Branding her, claiming her. I want her to look in the mirror for the rest of her life and know that she belongs right here with me.

"If I don't have you right now, *I* will go insane."

"We can't, we—"

I silence her with another filthy kiss, dragging on her bottom lip with my teeth. "I'm going to need you to stop fussing and start concentrating on how you're going to get your pretty little mouth around my cock."

She whimpers at my words, submitting herself entirely to the arms that have wrapped themselves around the small of her back.

"Come here," I say as I help her onto the bed. Her knees land on either side of my waist so that she's straddling me properly.

Her head dips down to kiss me again, giving me a delightful eyeful down her shirt. My fingers begin to work the buttons open of their own accord.

She does the rest of the work for me, shrugging out of the material as she sucks crudely on my tongue. It's a demonstration of what's to come.

Yet she's still careful, still gentle with her touches, cautious not to jostle me too much as she makes sinful noises against my mouth and grinds down on my hardening cock. It would be infuriating if it weren't so fucking thoughtful.

She withdraws suddenly to continue the path of kisses down my torso, and it feels like she takes the air with her.

My hand clasps her wrist to get her to stop, and she looks up in confusion.

"You first."

Her pupils dilate as she licks her lips. "I'm not sure—"

"Sit on my fucking face, Mia."

She doesn't need to be told again, shuffling up my body

instead of down and sliding her panties off in the process. Her skirt rides all the way up her waist.

"That's a good girl," I hum my approval against her thigh. "Doesn't it feel good to do as you're told?"

She whimpers slightly as my tongue darts across her skin.

"Hold onto the headboard with both hands," I instruct her as she hovers tentatively over me. My breath tickles her core, and I can practically taste the wetness that has already accumulated there.

"Let me taste you."

She sits with a noise of surrender, and I immediately gorge myself on her fruit.

It's thick and needing and wanting and oh, so eager for attention. I lick along her entirely, stopping only to pay special attention to her sensitive clit, circling it lightly over and over so that my tongue almost feels as if it were vibrating.

The results are glorious, and I'm rewarded with movement. Mia's hips grind against my face as I greedily offer my tongue for friction.

Nothing has ever tasted so good. Nothing ever will.

My hands dig into her ass cheeks hard enough to bruise as I let her chase her pleasure endlessly.

I know the second my tongue stops being enough. Her hands leave the headboard and yank at my hair.

I withdraw entirely. "Put your hands back on the headboard."

"Leon," never has my name sounded so beautiful than on her half-broken lips. "Please. I need you. I need more."

"I know what you need," I lick her hard, and her back

arches back. "I'm going to give it to you. But your hands need to be back on the headboard."

I make sure to praise her when she deliriously complies. "So receptive to me, aren't you? So good at following orders."

I reward her with another lick before returning to her clit. She moans in protest, too distracted to notice my middle finger at her entrance until I've plunged into her past the knuckle.

"Oh, fuck!" she cries as I begin to work her hard. My mouth never leaves her sensitive clit, sucking at it while I fuck her with my finger. Then with two.

Then, as my fingers curl inside her, I draw out a groan from her that practically rattles through the room. The thighs around my face begin to tremble, and my mouth replaces my fingers to fuck her one last time with my tongue.

She comes undone on top of me, and I relish every moment of it.

Finally, she dismounts, chest heaving. My hands trail after her, desperate not to be subjected to her absence.

"I need you," she pants as she moves down the bed. "I need you in my mouth right now."

I watch in near-stupefied wonder as the woman makes short work of my pants and frees me from my too-tight boxers. She eyes up my length greedily before her tongue darts out to lick carelessly, bottom to top, her lips pressing lightly over my swollen end.

It's the most sinful thing I've ever seen.

"Fuck, Mia," I groan at those eyes. Those fucking *eyes* look up at me through hooded lids.

I try to burn the image into my memory.

She holds my gaze as she drops down, and my mind goes entirely blank.

Somewhere in the haze of my subconscious, I'm aware of her groaning around my cock. I'm aware of the way the sounds vibrate across my skin.

I'm aware that she can't swallow me whole, but she makes up for it with her hands wrapped around my base. I'm aware that her eyes water beautifully as she takes me to the very back of her throat.

A stronger man than me would have let this continue for hours. He would have basked in the glory of this moment for as long as humanly possible.

But I've never been a strong man when it comes to Maddison.

I grip her hair in warning, but she doesn't move an inch, swallowing down my undoing without even flinching as star-filled darkness threatens to cloud my vision.

She sits up on her forearms with a satisfied smirk that I want to kiss straight off her face.

"Satisfied, are you?" I ask, though my voice sounds entirely wrecked.

Mia's smile only grows as she hums happily, licking her lips. "I'm going to go clean up."

I groan petulantly. "Don't leave me."

"I'll be back in a minute."

She goes to stand, and I make a show of dramatically lying back down, listening to her feet pad into the ensuite as I let the euphoria settle all over my body.

It's never felt like this before.

No one has ever felt like Mia before.

That woman...this woman...my woman.

My wife.

Mine.

We could do this forever if we wanted. There could be something here beyond sex and obligation. It would be easy. There's no reason for us not to now, not when I already have my heart halfway through that particular door.

"Leon?"

"Come back to bed," I moan, missing her and missing her.

"*Leon.*"

I finally look up at her, and the smirk drops from my lips when I realize what she's holding.

"I'm pregnant."

19

MIA

The pregnancy test feels like lead in my hand. It's far too heavy for me to keep holding on to.

I hold it out to him, but he's still staring at me, his face unreadable.

The nerves kick in as the silence stretches.

Because it's my duty to sleep with him, my duty to provide an heir to the Prince's Hand. That was always the understanding we had; that's what I'd agreed to do.

But what we just did, completely and ruinously ill-advised by any medical professional, had nothing to do with creating an heir. It hadn't even crossed my mind.

The only goal was to feel. And I've never felt more. It was everything.

And everything feels overwhelming in the face of reality. In the face of a positive pregnancy test and a tangible reminder as to why we are both even here in the first place.

"Are you sure?" These are his first words, none bearing even a fraction of the emotion of a few moments ago.

I swallow hard. "I...I should do another. I'll book an appointment in the morning just in case."

Leon suddenly rises to his feet, his nakedness entirely distracting when I really need to focus on what he's saying for my own sanity. "No."

"We need to make sure."

"You won't leave this house," he says evenly. "I'll have a doctor come visit."

I open my mouth and close it again. Let out an equally even breath. "I'm perfectly capable of visiting the clinic myself."

"There's no need, not anymore." Leon takes a step forward.

He's close enough now that I can see the intensity in his eyes. There's clarity there that had been absent when his cock was in my mouth. I miss that look of haziness with a pang of unwarranted desire.

I shake my head. "Well, I have to leave at some point. You can't plan on keeping me locked in here until I give birth."

He says nothing. He steps closer.

My arms wrap around my chest, suddenly very, very wary. "Leon?"

"That's exactly what I intend to do."

"You can't be serious." It comes out in a whisper instead of a statement of defiance.

Leon looms before me, his strong shoulders bearing the weight of an entire mafia family, and I realize with a dreadful lurch in my stomach exactly what's about to happen.

"You bear my child," he says. "It is now my duty to keep you safe."

"Your duty?" The words are bitter on my tongue. Because, of course, this is what it all comes down to.

"Mia."

Not Mia. Not anymore.

Because it might have been fun to flirt with me, fun to fuck me. Fun to dance up against me in a club where no one could see us. But now that I've served my purpose...

"No, you're right," I swallow hard as I take a step back. "Let's not lose sight of what's important here. I wouldn't want anything to distract from bearing your goddamn children."

His eyebrows knit into a tight frown. "You know how important this is."

"I don't need you to remind me!" I laugh even though I feel like crying. "Is that everything you want from me this evening? Have I fulfilled my purpose? Can your wife return to bed so that she might rot there in peace?"

"I'm not sending you away." He suddenly crowds me again. "I want you to stay."

How many times has he asked that of me now? Each request had been like a jolt of electricity to the heart, a whisper of something more that could flourish behind it.

Now it just sounds like...

Stay where I can see you. Stay so you don't wander too far. Stay so that I can know you're safe.

Stay safe. Stay safe.

It's my duty to stay safe.

"Why?" I ask because my heart is already breaking.

His expression shifts into alarm. He wasn't expecting me to ask.

I want to scream at him, want to beg him. *Please, give me one good reason. Please tell me there's something more. Please.*

There's more, isn't there? You feel this, too. You can't kiss me like that, make me feel *like that, if you don't feel it. I need more.*

"I'm sorry." He searches my face for something I evidently don't provide. "You can leave if you want to."

It feels worse than when Amos Rubio kicked me in the chest. "Right."

I back away before I can say something I regret. Or my body betrays me with some gross display of emotion that I can already feel simmering under the surface.

"I didn't mean to..." Leon trails off when I look back at him. He swallows the words back down, chocolate eyes burning with an emotion I can't name. "Goodnight, Mia."

I don't trust myself to voice a reply.

I slip out through the door and into the room that I've never slept in before.

THE WALLS of the brownstone feel closer every day, the once-grand space shrinking into a prison with every passing hour.

I've memorized every detail of it—the cracks in the kitchen countertops where Leon had once bent me over. The subtle creak of the third step on the staircase, the way the light filters through the heavy curtains in the living room just before dusk.

I can't remember the last time I felt the fresh air on my face or the hum of the city beneath my feet.

At first, I thought I could handle it. I thought I could just stay quiet and fulfill my goddamn duty.

But after three weeks, I had gone to Leon after a dreadful morning of sickness and begged him. I pleaded with him to let me out. To give me *something*.

"I'm keeping you safe," he had said the last time I brought it up, his voice calm but final, his hand brushing over my stomach. Making it very clear who, exactly, he's trying to keep safe.

The child growing inside me should be a blessing. Instead, it feels like a leash.

That was the day I decided to leave. I ran down the stairs, my feet making the third step creak, and burst through the front door. For a moment, I just let the sounds of the city overwhelm me.

Then I saw that Max was stationed outside. He turned me back around with a sympathetic look of a man on someone else's payroll.

Leon's absence only sharpens the edges of my isolation. At first, his injury kept him home. But once he was mobile again, he threw himself back into his world of business and violence, leaving me behind to rot in silence.

Well, not complete silence.

"I don't know how you tolerate that shade of paint," Isabella says, eyeing the soft gray walls of the study with disdain as she scrolls through an iPad.

I don't answer her. Instead, I sip my mint tea (the only warm beverage I can tolerate at the moment) and try not to let her snide comments get under my skin.

It's become a near-daily battle now that we're making some headway on the casino. But, ironically, it's one of the only ways I've managed to stay sane.

The workload piles up every time Isabella visits, and my life revolves around completing it before she returns.

I pour myself into every detail of the casino, pouring over layouts, reviewing color schemes, and fine-tuning the marketing strategy. If Leon won't let me leave this house, I'll make damn sure I leave my mark on something outside of it.

"You should approve these floor plans for the third floor this week," she says, sliding the tablet toward me. "Otherwise, we'll have to delay the scaffolding."

Her tone is sharp and businesslike, but I catch the hint of sympathy in her eyes. As if she is realizing she might be the only person her brother even allows to visit.

"I'll do it," I say, because I will. Because I have nothing better to do.

I spend my mornings reviewing invoices and liaising with contractors via email. Afternoons are devoted to drafting proposals—VIP memberships, themed rooms, and entertainment lineups.

Evenings are the hardest.

The house is too quiet, and the ache of loneliness settles in my chest like a weight I can't shake. Some nights, I sit by the window and stare out at the city, wondering if Leon even remembers I'm here.

It's not just Leon's absence that eats at me. It's the silence between us when he's here, the way he looks at me with something that feels less like love and more like obligation.

He wanted an heir, I remind myself bitterly, *not a partner. He wants me to stay right here. Until the baby is born and he has no use for me anymore.*

More often than not, I spend my evenings thinking of his other self. The one who offered desperate kisses and longing moans and words that praised me and pushed me over the edge of my own control.

The man who graces me with his presence only to dart back out of it at his earliest opportunity is nothing like the man who had held me that night.

Deception & Desire

I can see it on his face, the exhaustion that lines his every expression. This is a man built for war, a man able to continue on nothing more than fumes. There's no life there anymore, just action and firm words and practical solutions.

By the time I'm ready for my twenty-two week scan, we feel almost like strangers.

"Lie down whenever you're ready," the pre-approved doctor tells me as I drop down onto the bed.

Leon had brought up all the equipment necessary to do my checkups personally, as if worried it might spontaneously explode if he didn't check it all over himself. Now, the ultrasound machine hums non-threateningly in my ear as the doctor lifts up my shirt.

"There," the sonographer says, angling the screen toward us.

Leon automatically sits beside me, his hand finding mine, solid and steady.

The image of a tiny, perfect profile appears on the monitor, and my breath catches. I've seen ultrasounds before in books and movies, but nothing compares to this—to seeing *our* baby.

"And here's baby number two," the sonographer continues casually.

Leon's grip tightens on my hand. "Two?" he echoes.

The sonographer smiles, nodding. "Twins. Two healthy heartbeats."

She adjusts the wand, and I see it: two tiny shapes nestled together in perfect harmony.

My chest tightens, and tears blur my vision. I glance at Leon, expecting his usual calm composure, but his face is anything but. His mouth is slightly open, his eyes wide and glassy, unguarded in a way I've never seen.

"Twins," he murmurs, almost to himself. He leans closer to the screen, his hand trembling in mine.

The sight of his rare vulnerability breaks something loose inside me. The tears come harder, and the words spill out before I can stop them.

"Leon, I can't stay locked away anymore. I need to breathe. Please."

He tears his eyes away to look at me; shock and sorrow and pure, unfiltered longing echo across his face.

"It's okay." An arm around my shoulder, holding me. I crave it like nothing else. "I've got you."

"This is important," I half choke on the word. "I want to share it. I want Cas to know, Isabella. My dad. Leon, please. I need to feel human again, I need to get out of here and I need to see them. Let me...let me have a baby shower."

He doesn't answer right away, his gaze fixed on the screen. Then, slowly, he turns to me, his eyes damp.

"A baby shower," he says softly, his thumb brushing over my knuckles so gently. "For you three, anything. A small one. Our family, our people."

Relief crashes over me as I cling to his hand like it could anchor me to my sanity.

"Anything, Mia. I promise."

20

LEON

I've never had the opportunity to host at the Brownstone beyond the occasional visit from Teo or Isabella. And, of course, Mia, but considering she legally owns the place, it doesn't feel like it counts. Besides, she's spent more time here than I have.

Needless to say, she already has a half dozen plans for decorating, compiling a list of "necessities" that are non-negotiable and needed *immediately.*

But who am I to deny her a thing?

For the first time in months, my woman was blazing brightly. Her swollen stomach was soft and protruding perfectly over her hips, carrying our children, instilling her with a glow that seemed to become more beautiful by the day.

Twins. The moment I saw them at the check-up, heard their fragile little heartbeats, I knew I would burn the world for them. All three of them.

"I'm going to stretch the perimeter out by another

block," Dante says as he sticks his head into the living room on his way out the door.

The party isn't due to start for another hour, but both he and Max arrived early to help establish security. Neither have seen fit to comment on my paranoia, which would be unusual had we not been dealing with the Cartel these last few months.

They were both there at The Inferno. *None* of us had anticipated an ambush like that. None of us thought Amos Rubio was reckless enough to put himself out into the field.

But what was worse—especially in terms of feeding that seemingly infectious paranoia—is the fact we've barely heard a thing from them since.

Not for lack of trying.

I've spent weeks scouring the streets for even a lowly henchman from Rubio's team. But it's like the entire operation has simply vanished into smoke.

Our lead on the private property shipments has all but dried up. No one has been seen entering or leaving the Rubio mansion to the point that we've been theorizing about tunnels. Even the progress we were making on the hydrogen bombs came to a standstill.

It's as if they're intentionally trying to psyche us out.

Which means we're all on high alert for whatever their next move will be.

"Security updates?" I turn to Max, who's been pacing the room like a caged tiger.

"Dante and I swept all the floors twice," Max replies. "No sign of trouble, and no one's getting in or out without our say-so. Teo's men are in place. This house is perhaps the safest place in the entire country."

"Good," I mutter, but my jaw stays tight.

I shouldn't have even considered this. Having so many prominent figures in one place was too risky, but...

For weeks, Mia has been a ghost, fading into the background of every room she inhabits as if she isn't entirely real.

I need to breathe.

I'd been so caught up in keeping her safe that I hadn't realized I was suffocating her. It's a necessary evil, one that I can't bring myself to regret. Not when it means that our *children* are alive and healthy.

And yet...

She deserves this. She deserves to see the people who care about her. She deserves to smile again, to laugh, to find joy in this house that must feel like a glorified prison.

But my instincts rebel at the thought of letting my guard down for even a moment.

The first guests arrive just as I'm triple-checking the living room windows. I have to stop myself from drawing the curtains despite the fact it's the middle of the day.

Cassandra walks in with her husband, Rocco. I haven't seen either of them since the wedding, and the air between us suddenly becomes tense. These are Mia's people, not mine.

Rocco, for all his talk of retirement, still carries himself like a soldier as he approaches. "Leon," he greets me, shaking my hand. "Still the over-prepared type, I see."

"You caught all that? I thought you were supposed to be retired," I reply simply.

He smirks. "I'm on sabbatical."

Further conversation is interrupted by the arrival of Isabella and Teo, who ease the tension with warm greetings and hugs between the women.

I almost don't notice Marco slipping in. Mia's father is dressed sharply and already heading for a glass of whiskey, as if that might do anything to ease the nerves of facing his daughter's wrath.

It's not my place to intervene. However, a part of me hates the man for causing her such unnecessary strife. The same part that hates him hates me, too.

And then, she arrives.

Mia steps into the room, her hand immediately going to rest lightly on Cassandra's arm. Her presence is commanding and soft all at once, causing the room to seemingly swell all around her.

She's wearing a simple black dress that blows out over her now-quite-noticeable bump. Her hair is swept up to expose the curve of her neck.

For a moment, I can't breathe.

It's not the dress or her smile, though both are stunning. It's the light in her shockingly green eyes, the way she stands taller as if she's reclaiming a part of herself I thought I'd stolen.

I step toward her without realizing it, my feet moving on instinct.

"Leon," she says softly as if I hadn't just interrupted her conversation. Her voice is like a balm and a dagger.

"You're...you look beautiful," I manage, and it feels like the most honest thing I've said in months.

Cassandra's eyes flicker between us knowingly. "She does, doesn't she? It's that pregnancy glow, I think. I'm so jealous, you know. When I was carrying Cory..."

She carries on talking, but all I hear is the attentive chuckle that escapes Mia's lips. All I can see is the way she tucks a strand of wine-red hair behind her ear, as if I haven't been twitching to do it for her since the moment she entered the room.

I clear my throat. "Excuse me."

For the rest of the night, I'm distracted. Teo speaks to me about Guild operations. I nod, but my attention drifts to Mia. Isabella tries to goad me into teasing Marco about his drinking. I brush her off, my gaze glued to Mia as she laughs with Cas.

Even as I exchange pleasantries with Rocco, my mind is on her.

My Mia. My wife. My family.

Tonight, she is surrounded by people who love her, and for the first time in a long time, she looks free.

Mia clears her throat, stepping toward the center of the room. The quiet hum of conversation dies down as everyone turns to her.

I can feel her nerves as if they were my own, see the way she clutches her hands together, and my chest tightens. I want to go to her, shield her from the weight of all those eyes, but I stay rooted where I am. This is her moment.

"I just wanted to say thank you," she begins, her voice soft but steady. "For being here today. It means the world to me that you'd take a moment away from the insanity of your lives to celebrate something so small."

"We love you, Mia!" Cas heckles, earning a ripple of laughter from the room.

She smiles at her oldest friend gratefully. "I know this hasn't been the most conventional situation, and for the part I played in making it necessary...I'm sorry."

Her gaze flickers over to Teo and then her father before she steadies herself once more.

"But today is about celebrating good news." Her gaze

finally lands on me, and I feel the heat of it all the way across the room. "And so, I have one last announcement to make."

Her words trail off as she places a hand on her belly, and suddenly, there's a mischievous glint in her eyes. "Leon and I are having twins."

A ripple of gasps and laughter spreads through the room. Cassandra squeals, Isabella claps, and Marco—even in his half-drunken stupor—grins like he's won the lottery.

But I can't hear any of it. My world narrows to Mia—her smile, her joy, the way she glows under the soft light.

My family.

My chest swells with so much emotion it's almost unbearable. I feel like the future isn't just a dark void but something bright and real, something worth fighting for.

"Boss."

Dante's voice cuts through my reverie, and I turn reluctantly, tearing my eyes away from Mia. He's standing at my side, his usual smirk replaced with something softer.

"Come on, man," he says, nudging me toward the corner of the room. "I know that look. You're totally gone for her. It's written all over your face."

I bristle instinctively, but Dante raises a hand. "Relax. I'm not here to give you grief. I just...I've seen you these past few months, Leon. Hell, we've all seen it. You've been fighting like a man with nothing left to lose. But now? Look at her. Look at what you have."

I glance back at Mia. She's laughing with Isabella and Cassandra, her hand still on her belly, the picture of happiness.

"You've got something rare," Dante continues, his voice

quieter. "And you don't get many chances at that in this life. Stop pushing her away. Go talk to her. Be happy, for once."

His words hit harder than I expected. Happiness feels like such an optimistic prospect; it barely feels like it could even be obtainable anymore.

But for Mia? For our family? Anything. I would do anything.

I nod, clapping a hand on Dante's shoulder. "Thanks."

But before I can take a step toward her, the room shifts.

The hum of conversation turns to murmurs, the air thickening with unease. And then—

The explosion hits.

21

MIA

My ears are ringing as I slowly come to my senses.

Vaguely, I'm aware I'm on the floor, back pressing into something hard and uncomfortable as I gasp for breath through the thick dust. The deafening sound of the explosion still echoes in my skull.

My hands instinctively fly to my stomach, protectively cupping it as I blink my eyes open.

Nothing makes sense. One moment, I was facing my family and my friends. Every person who ever meant something to me. The next, I'm staring up at the ceiling.

Whatever is left of it.

I stagger to my feet shakily, struggling to find my balance on the crumbling rubble.

The room around me is now a chaotic mess of fallen furniture, shattered glass, and splintered wood. The walls are cracked, the windows blown out. The decorations I'd insisted on now lie limply on the floor.

Where is Leon?

I can barely see through the haze, but the screams and cries of panic pierce through my confusion. I blink, trying to clear my vision, my heart hammering in my chest.

"Leon!" My voice breaks, the word choking me, but it doesn't matter. There's no response.

I push forward, carefully avoiding broken glass and debris, my hand still holding tight to my belly. The twins are moving, restless under my hands, and I can't help but wonder if they feel the same terror I do.

The tears come without warning, sliding down my face as I stumble over the wreckage. I can't think straight, the fear clouding my mind, but I force myself to focus. I have to find my family.

And then I see her.

Cassandra's lifeless form is buried under a pile of rubble near the far side of the room. My stomach lurches.

No.

I rush to her, my legs unsteady beneath me, and kneel beside the mess of debris.

Cassandra's pale face is smeared with dirt and blood, her body crushed beneath a heavy piece of the wall. Her arm is twisted awkwardly, and I can't see her breathing.

"Cas? Cas! Talk to me. Come on, Cas. Please," I whisper, my hands trembling as I try to lift the rubble.

I shouldn't be strong enough to move the concrete alone, but the sheer desperation of my adrenaline fuels me. Before I can really register what I'm doing, I'm pulling the last piece of debris away.

"Cas? Cassandra, don't you dare. Come on," I whimper as I search for a pulse.

There. Finally. Relief floods through me as I feel life flickering through her veins. She's breathing, she's alive.

A sob escapes my chest.

"Cassandra," I whisper again, louder this time, my hands gently cradling her head.

Her eyelids flicker, and after a moment, she groans, her hand weakly grasping mine.

"Mia..." she murmurs, her voice hoarse. "What...what happened?"

I shake my head, wiping my face with the back of my hand. "A bomb or something. But you're alive. Thank God you're alive."

Cassandra's hand weakly grips mine. "Where...where's Rocco? Where's Leon?"

My heart skips a beat, panic rising in my chest once more. I swallow hard, trying to steady my breath. "I don't know. We need to find them."

I look around the room, trying to pierce through the dusty smog that has engulfed the space. There are voices and signs of life, but they're indistinguishable through the ringing in my ears.

"Can you stand?" I ask Cassandra, helping her to sit up as I try to keep the panic from overtaking me.

She nods, though she looks dazed, her face pale and bruised. "I think so."

"Stay close," I tell her, my voice shaking. "We'll find them. We'll find everyone."

We move together, carefully stepping through the rubble, clinging to each other like a lifeline. My heart pounds in my chest, my eyes scanning the wreckage for any sign of Leon.

"Leon!" I call again, but my voice feels small in the

wreckage, swallowed by the smoke and dust.

Cassandra's hand tightens around mine as if to comfort me. I don't think anything of it until I realize she's stopped moving entirely.

"Cas, come on. We need to—"

My voice trails off the second I realize what she's staring at. My eyes open wide and flood with unshed tears.

"No."

There, buried under the rubble only a few feet away, is an arm. It's the only appendage not crushed by the giant slab of the ceiling.

And I know who it is immediately.

I've known that hand my whole life. The hand that held mine as a child, the hand that steadied my gun at the shooting range. The hand that wrapped around my arm the day I was to be married.

"No."

Everything crumbles apart.

I'd rather take a knife to the gut. I'd rather the ceiling had crushed me instead.

I immediately mentally apologize to my children. Everything is different now, but that doesn't stop my heart from breaking into thousands of pieces.

"Daddy, no."

It wasn't fair. I hadn't forgiven him yet. We were supposed to have years to rebuild, years to figure out how to trust each other again.

Now, all I have is endless guilt that wails from my throat like a siren.

Cas falls to her knees beside me. I don't know when I dropped to the floor, but her arms wrap around me now.

Protective, reassuring. Holding me together with her bare hands as I wail and wail.

"Mia!"

The voice cuts through my grief like a knife.

"Mia, where are you?" The relief in Leon's voice almost makes me start wailing again. I look up frantically, searching.

And then, there he is.

Leon strides toward us, his face bloodied, bruises already forming. But his eyes are crystal clear as he scans the room.

When he sees me, it's as if the world falls away, leaving only us.

Before I can take a breath, he's there, on his knees, pulling me into his arms. His hands cup my face, his touch so urgent, so frantic. He pulls back, eyes scanning me, looking for any sign of injury.

"You're okay," he breathes, his voice rough. "Are you hurt? The twins—are you—"

"My dad," my voice breaks. "Leon."

I see the moment he realizes as the grief floods his expression. It's too much. I bury my head into his chest.

He strokes my hair as I cling to him. "I'm sorry. I'm so sorry."

"I didn't get to tell him. I–I still loved him."

"He knew," he says with such authority I almost choke. "It's okay, Mia. He knew. He did."

He gently lowers his hand to my stomach, his touch tender and sweet. The twins are still moving; the soft flutter of life beneath my skin grounds me back into the moment.

My grief needs to wait. Our home is destroyed. There

could be more to this attack than just an explosion. We're not out of the woods yet.

Luckily, Cas is slightly more put together than I am. "What happened, Leon? Where is everyone else?"

Leon places a firm kiss on my forehead before pulling away and turning to address my friend. "A bomb, I think. It must have been planted somewhere upstairs. It should have been impossible."

"Rocco?" Cas' voice breaks.

"He's alive, Cassandra," Leon says gently before getting to his feet, holding an arm out to each of us. "Come on. We need to get out of here."

It takes us a moment to find our footing again, but then Cas is running, shouting for a husband like a woman possessed.

Leon's arm wraps around my waist, helping me over every minor obstacle in my path. I lean desperately into his touch and take as much reassurance from it as I can as we clear the room and stumble out into the foyer.

The entire house looks like it's been through an earthquake. Cracks have appeared up the walls, lighting fixtures have crashed into the floor. The glass of the Caravaggio has smashed into a thousand pieces and lies half torn beneath its previous spot on the wall.

But nothing is more harrowing than the expressions of the people who turn to look at us.

Rocco is already embracing his wife, while Teo and Isabella cling to each other desperately. Dante and Max are both on the floor—Max is suffering from a gruesome-looking head wound that Dante is attempting to bandage.

Each of them turns to look at Leon with a chilling sense

of expectation. There's anger in their faces, desperation. Pain.

I realize with a start that they're looking to their leader.

And Leon Natali was forged for war.

"We retaliate," Leon says, his voice now cold, as he steps forward. His hand lingers on my waist as if to reassure himself that I'm still there. "We go to war."

It's Isabella who speaks up first, eyes frantic with fear. "We don't know anything yet. We don't know who this was for sure."

"They attacked my home. They attacked my pregnant wife. They attacked my *family*. There is no more room for waiting around and playing this safe. As of right now, The Prince's Hand is at war with the Cartel," Leon's voice booms out with authority.

As his words sink in, he turns to Teo and Rocco. "Is the Guild with me?"

Teo shares a long look with Rocco. Their faces are grim with the same resolve that has defined them all these years.

"Of course," Teo says, his voice laced with the same anger I can see burning in Leon's eyes.

"I guess my sabbatical is officially over," Rocco mutters over Cas' head.

I sag against Leon's arm and listen to him bark out instructions, the adrenaline finally starting to wear off and the exhaustion kicking with a vengeance. I don't realize how close I am to toppling over before Leon suddenly catches me.

"I'm fine," I say to the frown on his face.

Leon's chocolate-colored eyes are everywhere, darting across my body as if he can somehow do a comprehensive medical analysis by sight alone.

I expect him to chastise me, to hit me with some insistence that I rest.

I don't expect him to bark for Teo. "I need a favor, Vitale."

The Guild's don enters my periphery with a concerned look at me. "What do you need?"

"I seem to recall that you have a bunker. I need Mia to stay somewhere safe until the babies are born."

22

LEON

The Cartel's blood seeps into Brooklyn's streets like a stain that refuses to lift.

After four months, even the local broadcasters are getting wind of "extensive gang activity", warning civilians to stay home at night, suggesting curfews for their own safety.

I have no interest in civilians. I have no interest in the Cartel's goons either.

The only blood I long for is Amos Rubios.

I've turned the borough into a chessboard, every block a battleground, every move calculated to deliver maximum pain.

They thought the explosion would cripple us. They were wrong. I prove it to them every time they seek us out, every time I annihilate everything in my path.

They brought this violence on themselves the second they attacked my family.

I don't stop. I don't sleep. I live in the Guild's warehouse, where we've set up a war office that can accommodate the combined forces of both Teo's men and mine.

Teo sits in the corner, surrounded by monitors, tapping away, looking at security feeds and encrypted servers. His knack for digital warfare is unmatched, and he finds the cracks in the Cartel's armor before they even know they've exposed themselves.

"Their shipment lands at Pier 27 tomorrow night," Teo says one evening, his voice flat but focused. "Weapons. High-end. Heavy."

I nod, already planning. "Rocco, get your people on the dockworkers' union. I want eyes and ears before they unload a single crate."

Rocco leans back in his chair, cracking his knuckles. "Done."

Dante handles the international angles, his connections running deep in shipping and logistics. When the Cartel reroutes their product through the ports in Jersey, Dante has their smugglers cornered before they even leave the harbor.

"We've got a freighter with their name on it," he tells me, his tone smug. "Offloaded on our doorstep by mistake. Shame, isn't it?"

Even Max, recovering from his head injury, refuses to sit idle. He spends most of his time glued to my side whenever I'm not out in the field myself, contributing where he can.

"We've cut off most of their resources now," he says one night, his voice still a little rough, one eye perpetually sagging under his wound. "It's only a matter of time before desperation weeds out their weaker foot soldiers. Rubio can't keep them paid."

But this war is more than tactics and alliances. It's a grind.

Months of bloodshed, back-and-forth battles, and neighborhoods turned into war zones. Businesses pay the price of our aggression. Families hide behind locked doors.

And through it all, I miss her.

Mia.

Four months of nothing but a hard cot and a dozen other men snoring in my ear, and I can still imagine her tucked beneath the blankets of my king-sized bed at the Brownstone.

Our bed.

My one reassurance is that she's safe, hidden in a bunker far from the chaos. She might hate me for it; likely, she'll never forgive me for locking her away again. But theirs are the three heartbeats that I refuse to put at risk.

But every day without her feels like a knife twisting in my chest. When the silence falls at the end of each long night, all I can think about is her voice, her touch.

I think of the way she used to look at me in those brief moments when I thought we could be something important.

"Heads up." Rocco drags me from my brooding to draw my attention back to the war room. "Teo's found something."

The Cartel pushes back harder every week, desperate and cornered.

But I push harder.

When they try to open a new drug route through Brighton Beach, I have Max and Dante shut it down before the ink on their contracts dries. When they threaten one of Teo's cyber operatives, Rocco has the man relocated and safe within hours.

Move. Countermove.

But no matter how many victories I win, the weight

never lifts. Not when every choice I make seems to drive us deeper into the trenches. When every success leads me further from Mia.

Yet I cling to a notion, a plan that's been weeks in the making. Every detail, every contingency, is hammered out with precision.

I don't leave anything to chance—this isn't just about winning. It's about crushing the Cartel so thoroughly that Amos Rubio has no choice but to retreat to his fortress. One blow big enough to corner him for good. The beginning of the end.

Teo finally joins us at the table, spreading out the maps he's been working on before us—the Cartel's remaining operations are like a spiderweb stretched across the city.

"They've centralized," he says as he taps at the map. "One location, high risk, higher security. They're desperate."

"Good. That makes them predictable."

Our target is a sprawling warehouse, one of the last major hubs the Cartel controls in Brooklyn. It's more than a storage site; it's their final lifeline. Drugs, weapons, cash—all of it flows through that building.

"We hit it hard and fast," Dante says as he peers over the map behind Teo. "Take it out, and they'll fold."

"Not just fold," I correct him. "We want Rubio on his knees."

ON THE NIGHT of the attack, the air is electric.

Rocco secures our entry point through his contacts in the docks. Max oversees the strike team, coordinating with Dante to handle extraction. Teo monitors everything from his command center, relaying updates to keep us one step ahead.

My men move like shadows, slipping through the dark streets surrounding the warehouse. From my vantage point on a nearby rooftop, I watch as the Cartel's guards patrol the perimeter, their arrogance palpable.

They don't see it coming.

It begins with a single explosion—atTeo's signal. A fuel truck parked along the warehouse ignites in a massive fireball, throwing the guards into chaos. My men move in immediately, breaching the building within seconds.

I'm on the ground with them, leading the charge. My gun is steady in my hand, every shot purposeful. I don't waste time or ammunition. Each Cartel soldier that stands in our way falls quickly, their defenses crumbling under the weight of our assault.

"Save some for the rest of us," Dante barks a laugh as he dispatches a man on my left with a flourishing gesture of his knife.

"This isn't a damn game."

The body slumps to the floor at my feet before Dante replies again. "That makes six. How many did you get?"

I point my gun over his shoulder and shoot the man inches away from tackling Dante from behind. "Thirteen."

The warehouse is a maze of crates and machinery. We had prepared for this, running through the schematics a hundred times. But no amount of preparation could have prepared me for the heaviness of the air, thick with smoke and adrenaline.

I can barely make out Max as he leads a group to secure the northern exit. Dante disappears at my side, too. His team pushes south, cutting off any escape routes.

I'm left to monitor my own team, still picking off the stragglers that were standing guard, waiting for the all-clear from Max and Dante.

When it comes, I don't hesitate.

We storm the central storage area, where lingering Cartel goons desperately attempt to shove duffle bags into heavily fortified SUVs, scrambling to regroup to face their imminent demise.

The sound of gunfire and shouts fills the air, but we don't relent. My team presses forward, refusing to yield to the pressure of their incoming fire. I can practically see the fear in their eyes when they realize we aren't ducking for cover.

I shoot brazenly, drawing as much fire as possible, taking a shot to the chest that punches into my bulletproof vest with the force of a bus. But still, I keep pushing us forward.

I'm a ruthless distraction if ever there was one.

I'm buying Max and Dante enough time to circle back. Within minutes, we have them entirely surrounded.

It's with no small amount of satisfaction that I watch the remaining guards either surrender or flee into the night. Their loyalty to the Cartel shattered in one ruthless night.

"Secure the perimeter," I command, stepping over a body as I make my way to the office at the back of the building.

Inside, I find exactly what I'm looking for: ledgers, shipment schedules, and stacks of cash. Evidence that ties Amos Rubio directly to every crime he's committed in Brooklyn.

"Boss," Teo's voice crackles through the comms. "Rubio's on the move. He's retreating back to the mansion. We've got him cornered."

I allow myself a brief, grim smile.

"Good," I say. "Now it's only a matter of time before—"

"LEON."

My head snaps up at the sound of Isabella's voice. She runs into the office, panting hard as she all but falls at my feet.

"What the *hell* are you doing here, Issy?" I'm yelling, out of fear or maybe outrage. I'm not entirely sure which.

Isabella remains unfazed, grabbing hold of my arm urgently and tugging me to my feet. "It's Mia."

All sense of victory immediately shatters at my feet.

"What?"

"Leon, she's gone into labor."

23

MIA

I clutch my swollen belly, inhaling deeply as another contraction ripples through me.

The twins are ready, which means that I should be ready.

Except I feel anything but.

"Okay, just lie back here and keep breathing for me." The doctor moves around me, her voice calm and steady, but I barely register her words.

My mind is elsewhere, still trapped in the endless hours of solitude. This doesn't feel real; it's as if it's happening to someone else entirely.

And the problem is, I understand why it had to be this way. From the snippets of information that Isabella has been able to get to me, the war has been brutal and dangerous, and absolutely no place for a pregnant woman.

I've had so much time to think about it. Hell, I've had too much time to think about all of it. And yes, I see the logic in keeping me out of harm's way.

But what about the father-to-be? What about the man who should be here right now?

A groan of pain worms itself out of my mouth as the contraction comes to a ruthless conclusion.

"There you go," the doctor praises me as I pant with my entire chest. "You're doing great. Drink some water, okay?"

It's just the two of us, but she's already prepared everything in the medical suite. I reach for the plastic cup eagerly, letting the cool liquid soothe the back of my aching throat.

I can endure this. If this is happening, if it's real. If I'm about to give birth in a bunker, miles away from everyone I love, I will endure it.

Because all I've done these last four months is endure. And this pain is temporary, but the grief I hold for my father will stay with me for the rest of my life.

I've endured the replaying of memories. The cadence of my father's laughter, the sternness of his absolute authority just waiting for me to undermine. The familiarity of his hands.

I'll never be able to hold them and tell him just how much I love him despite all of his flaws. I'll never be able to whisper that he could never do anything that would ever be enough for me to turn away from him forever.

He's gone.

Grief isn't sharp anymore. It's dulled, like an ache in old wounds, but it's constant.

"I don't want to be alone," I whisper, the words echoing the tragic voice of my lonely soul aren't meant for the doctor. But she reaches for my hand anyway.

"You are so brave. You're doing so well. I'm here. I'm not much, but you can pretend I'm whoever you need me to be."

And really, there's only one person I need to be here.

For months, I've tried to convince myself that our relationship doesn't matter, not in the face of everything else.

But the truth is, it does. The truth is, Leon has been important to me since the moment he kissed my hand at the altar.

And maybe it is one-sided. Maybe he's never seen me as anything more than a means to an end.

But I can't ignore the way I long for him now in my most desperate moments. I can't ignore the way I light up just at the memory of his touch. I can't forget that despite everything, despite my isolation, despite his absence, despite my father and a war and Amos Rubio....

I'm not going to stop loving him.

"Mrs. Natali," the doctor says gently, breaking through my thoughts. "We're up to four centimeters now. Things are moving quite quickly, okay? So take a breath whenever you can."

The contractions are closer together now, their intensity sharpening. I grip the edge of the bed, trying to steady my breathing, but my chest tightens with panic.

Does Leon even know?

He's been out there, fighting a war for months, risking his life to keep me safe.

Every day I've been in this bunker, I've feared the news of his death. Some nights, I've woken from nightmares where his bloodied body was the last thing I saw before the darkness swallowed me whole.

"Focus on your breathing," the doctor says, her hands on my arm.

I nod but don't answer. My thoughts are too loud, too chaotic.

Leon and I have been separated by more than just

distance. Too much is left unspoken, too many expectations have been thrust on our shoulders. Gentle moments have been overwhelmed by our responsibilities with not enough time to nurture anything more.

But none of that matters now. I just want him back. I want to see his face, to feel his hand in mine, to know he's alive.

A sharp pain rips through me, stealing my breath. The doctor starts giving instructions. Her tone is urgent but calm.

Leon, please. Come back to me. Don't die out there. Come back before it's too late.

The world is slipping away, my mind clouded with pain and exhaustion. Each contraction feels like a tidal wave dragging me under. My body is working against me, and I can barely keep up.

I squeeze my eyes shut, sweat dripping down my temples. My hands clutch at the sheets, desperate for something to anchor me. Somewhere in the haze, I hear the doctor's voice, calm and instructive, but it feels like it's meant for someone else.

Then I hear him.

"Mia. I'm here."

My eyes flutter open, unfocused at first, but then I see him—Leon.

His face is pale, his dark eyes filled with something I can't quite place, but the sight of him steadies me like nothing else could. I feel the tears leaking from my eyes.

"Leon?" My voice cracks.

"I'm here. I've got you." He kneels beside the bed, taking my hand in his.

His grip is firm and grounding, and his warmth cuts through the cold terror that has been gripping me for hours.

"Breathe for me, sweetheart. You're doing so well."

A sob wrenches from my mouth. I can't tell if it's from the pain or the sheer relief of seeing him.

"You're so strong," he whispers, his lips brushing against my temple. "You've always been strong, Mia. Just a little more, and we'll meet our babies. I'm so proud of you."

His words pull me back from the edge. I focus on his voice, his presence, and somehow, it makes the impossible seem bearable. I push through the pain, gripping his hand like a lifeline as the doctor urges me on.

"It's almost time," the doctor says.

Leon's lips find my ear, his voice trembling but steady. "You've got this. One more push. I'm right here. I'm right here. You're perfect, Mia. God, I've missed you so much."

With every ounce of strength I have left, I bear down. The pressure peaks, and then, suddenly, the room fills with a new sound—a cry, piercing and raw.

"It's a girl!" the doctor announces.

I gasp, my head falling back against the pillow as tears stream down my face. Leon presses his forehead to mine, his hand never leaving mine.

"She's beautiful," he whispers, his voice breaking.

But it's not over. Another contraction seizes me, and the process starts again. Leon doesn't waver. He stays by my side, whispering his praise through my painful delirium.

Minutes later, the second cry fills the room.

"And a boy!"

For a moment, the world feels still, the cries of our twins the only sound. Leon kisses my forehead, his hands cupping my face as he stares into my eyes.

"You did it," he says, his voice thick with emotion.

The doctor brings the twins to us, tiny and perfect, before swiftly tending to clean up.

Leon climbs onto the bed next to me so that they can settle between our arms. He looks at them like they're the most precious things in the world. "Hello," his voice breaks with emotion. "Hi."

"Look at them," I find myself choking out in amazement. "They're here. They're so real. Hello. Hello. I'm your mama. Hi baby, hi. This is your papa."

Leon turns back to me. He brushes a damp strand of hair from my face, his eyes shimmering. "This is our family."

I can feel my face crumpling under his gaze. "God, Leon. I want that so badly. Can you just...pretend for a moment? Please, I need you so much."

My hands reach up to wipe at my face, only to be captured gently by my wrists.

"Why would I pretend?" he says so softly. "I want this too. Mia, I've been in love with you for months. This is *it* for me."

My breath catches. "Stop it. Don't be cruel."

"My entire world is here on this bed. I don't want anything else."

My heart shatters and rebuilds in the same breath. Tears stream down my face as I reach for him, pulling him close.

"I can't lose you again," I whisper, my voice breaking. "Please, just stay."

"I will," he promises, his lips pressing softly to mine. "I will. Mia, please. Tell me, what are their names?"

I swallow back more tears as I gaze down at my two beautiful children.

"This is Elizabeth Rose," I kiss her forehead before turning to my son. "And this is Luca Marco."

24

LEON

In the aftermath of the attack on the Cartel warehouse and the birth of my children, things become...oddly gentle.

The war simmers rather than burns. Amos Rubio's retreat leaves cracks in the Cartel's operations that we quickly exploit. Closing in, one day after another, toward our final stand.

But it's work I've already planned ahead for. Teo continues to keep our territory secure as Rocco leads the push. Both have threatened me with grievous bodily harm if I decide to return to the field.

Allowing my focus to remain firmly on Mia and the babies.

Every day, I wake with a single purpose: to ensure my family is safe and thriving. The twins sleep soundly in their cribs—tiny, perfect reminders of a future beyond this chaos—and Mia, my Mia, is slowly recovering.

I hover over her constantly.

At first, she was too weak to protest, and I took full

advantage, bringing her meals, fluffing pillows, sitting beside her as she fed Liza and Luca.

If she frowned at me for being too attentive, I didn't care. I'm making up for lost time, for every moment I wasn't there when she needed me.

She's always been so strong, so fiercely independent. Watching her lean on me, even a little, is humbling. She claims to hate it, but I want desperately to earn back what I lost, to be worthy of her trust again.

To prove that this time, we can *both* stay.

"You're looking at me funny," she bemoans from her perch on the couch. She's not even looking at me, her nose firmly between the pages of a book while the twins sleep soundly in the next room.

I smirk to myself as I continue to breathe her in. She's pale, still recovering, but there's a light in her eyes that sings of that foreign concept: happiness.

The babies are eleven days old. Eleven days since my love confession was wrenched out of me in a moment of beautiful vulnerability that I don't regret for a second.

Only, we haven't talked about it since, dancing around each other with gentle words and touches, holding on to each other during those rare moments of peace when the two newborns aren't demanding our attention.

There's an understanding between us now, an acknowledgment that there is something so very important between us. But it also feels like we're in the endgame of a relationship we never really properly started.

It's all backward; marriage and kids came first.

So, I like to take advantage of these rare moments alone as much as I can.

"How are you feeling today?" I say as I cross the room and kneel beside her chair.

She gives me a small smile, though I can tell she's trying to downplay her fatigue. "Better," she says softly, her fingers reaching to tangle themselves in mine.

I nod, stroking her hand with my thumb. "You've been amazing, Mia. You deserve to be better."

She laughs lightly. "That's your way of telling me to rest more, isn't it?"

"Always," I admit, smiling. "But that's not why I'm here."

Her eyebrow quirks up, and she closes her book. "What's wrong?"

"Nothing bad," I say to soothe the worry on her face. "In fact, this will all be over soon. We have Rubio cornered now; his people are off the streets."

"Why am I hearing a *but*?"

"Actually, you're hearing a *moreover*," I tease back. "We would like to send out a message of power. And what better way to demonstrate the successful union of the Italian Mafia than through a monument to our collective strengths?"

Mia blinks at me as her brain catches up. "You want to open the casino."

"I want to open *your* casino." I lift her hand to my lips and kiss it softly. "Will you be my date to the opening?"

Her lips part slightly, surprise flickering across her face before she smiles—a genuine, radiant smile that feels like sunlight after a storm.

"I'd like that," she says.

When the car pulls to a stop outside the Prince's Hand casino, I'm out first, extending my hand to her like some lovesick schoolboy.

She takes it, and when she steps out, the sight of her in the glow of the casino's grand entrance leaves me momentarily speechless.

She's breathtaking in a deep emerald dress—the soft, fitted fabric that skimming her body and shimmering under every flicker of light. Her fiery hair cascades over her shoulders in a shining wave.

I can't take my eyes off her. I can't keep my *hands* off her.

A tug on her waist, my lips pressed to her temple. I can't stop touching her. "You're stunning."

Her cheeks flush, and she pulls away, but the corner of her mouth quirks into a small smile. "I'm postpartum. You have to say that. Otherwise, I'm legally required to murder you."

"No," I say, guiding her hand to my arm as we make our way up the steps. "It's you. You've always looked stunning to me. But in that dress...you've left me no chance of focusing on anything else tonight."

She doesn't respond, but her blush deepens, and it gives me hope—a flicker of a promise of something more.

But all thoughts leave the second we step through the front doors.

Inside, the casino is alive.

We enter the main floor, the sounds of shuffling chips, laughter, and clinking glasses spilling over us. It's dazzling and opulent. Painstaking attention to detail is realized in every sanded edge, warmly lit corner, and seamless transition of space.

Mia hesitates, her fingers tightening on my arm as she takes it all in.

"Perfect, isn't it?" I ask, leaning close enough that my voice is just for her.

"It's beautiful."

I can't resist another kiss to her temple. "I wouldn't go that far. Not with you standing right here."

She hits me playfully on the shoulder as someone approaches. Her sharp heels click against the polished floors.

"Mia," Isabella greets my wife first. I try not to look too surprised when she pulls her into a brief but genuine hug. "You look amazing. How do you like our little masterpiece?"

Mia laughs. "Little? This place has four separate thematic floors and a spa."

"I suppose we should go for eight next time, then."

Mia rolls her eyes at my sister, but my heart warms at the sight of them actually getting along.

We move through the room, greeting guests as we go. Teo and Dante are here, mingling with their usual charm, and Rocco and Cassandra wave from the bar.

Mia is gracious and poised, but I don't leave her side. I keep a hand on her waist or her back, drawn to her like gravity.

Whenever her laughter rings out, or her eyes meet mine, something in my chest tightens, and I dare to hope. Hope that by the end of the night, when it's just us again, I can hold her without fear of her slipping away.

For the most part, I know I should feel triumphant standing here, surrounded by power and allies, with Mia by my side. The war with the Cartel has almost reached its final, bloody conclusion, with victory very much in sight.

But I've never been one to relax. If I've learned one thing, it's that if things feel too good to be true, that's usually because they are.

I want to hate the part of me that tugs at the back of my mind, a sense that something isn't quite right. But it's kept me alive this long.

"Leon? Can I borrow you for a second?" Max calls from behind me. I turn to see him, his expression unusually grim as if he, too, can sense it. We've always been on a similar wavelength.

I glance back at Mia, where we're both standing with Isabella and Cassandra near the blackjack tables. She's smiling at something Isabella is saying as her gaze lands on me. A frown is already forming on my face as I hesitate.

"I'll only be a minute," I tell her, brushing my hand along her arm. She nods, and I follow Max toward a quieter corner.

"Talk to me," I say as soon as we're out of earshot.

"Just a feeling," he grimaces again before explaining himself, gesturing toward the floor. "Have you noticed the servers tonight?"

I frown, scanning the crowd.

At first, everything looks normal: well-dressed guests chat and laugh, and servers move seamlessly with trays of champagne flutes and hors d'oeuvres.

But then I see it: two servers exchanging a look that's too deliberate, their movements too calculated.

"What the hell?" I mutter, narrowing my eyes as another server, this one lingering near the craps table, subtly adjusts something at their waist. My instincts flare to life.

"Rubio is isolated. He doesn't have the resources to pull this off." I look around to gesture Teo over, but the don is nowhere to be found. "You filed the report, Max. This should be impossible, right?"

Max shifts at my side. "Yeah, unless I faked the report."

Time suddenly slows.

A glint of metal.

A gun.

It's pointed at me.

I turn to Max, the man who's been at my side for the better part of the year, the man who has stepped up at every available opportunity to prove his worth.

Now he's holding a gun to my face.

"Max," I say, my voice low and sharp. "What the hell are you doing?"

Suddenly, a lot of scattered pieces snap into place.

How Rubio had found out that Mia was my wife. How a bomb could be placed in the brownstone despite the relentless security checks. How a stranger from California could be so eager to be my second.

His expression is cool, detached, almost bored.

"Sorry, boss," he says, and the title drips with mockery. "But I've been playing this game a lot longer than you realize."

"Why?" I demand, my voice a growl.

"They made me a better offer, and let's be honest—you've been distracted. Love makes a man weak, Leon. And I don't follow weak leaders."

The betrayal cuts deep. Murderously deep. I trusted this man with my life. With my *wife*. But there's no time for it to fester, not now. Not when Mia is still on the floor, unknowingly surrounded by the enemy.

"Drop the gun."

Max smirks. "Consider this my formal resignation."

I react on pure instinct as he fires. The noise shatters the illusion of calm all around us. Someone screams.

Pain blossoms in my chest.

And then everything falls apart.

25

MIA

The gunshot cracks through the air, sharp and final. For a second, the room stills, the sparkling hum of the casino turning to stunned silence.

Then I see him.

Leon clutches his chest, blood seeping through his suit. His knees buckle, and he collapses, the shock on his face cutting me deeper than the chaos erupting around us.

"No!"

The scream tears from my throat as my body propels forward, shoving through the panicked crowd. My heart pounds, every instinct screaming to get to him, to make sure he's okay. He has to be okay.

God, please let him be okay.

I'm close, so close, when a hand clamps down on my arm.

I twist violently, coming face to face with a man dressed as a server. Except...no, how did the Cartel get in here? I thought Leon had them in retreat. No. No. No. This is all wrong.

"Let go of me!" I snarl, yanking my arm back, but his grip tightens, dragging me toward him.

A knife flashes in my face, and I lunge sideways, narrowly avoiding the blade.

He swings again, and I catch his wrist, using all my strength to push back. But he's bigger, stronger, and his other hand grabs for my neck.

Out of nowhere, a blur of movement crashes into him.

Isabella.

She moves with lethal precision, blonde and furious. Her fist connects with his jaw, and he stumbles. Before he can recover, she drives her knee into his stomach and twists the knife from his grip.

With one final strike, he crumples to the floor, unconscious.

"Get up," Isabella snaps as she offers me her hand. "We need to move now."

I stagger to my feet, still dazed, as someone else stumbles into us, eyes feral and wild, a broken champagne bottle clutched in her hand as if her life depends on it.

"Isabella! What's going on?" Cassandra gasps, her voice trembling.

"Cartel," Isabella says curtly, scanning the room. "Stay close. Fight if you have to."

The room is a battlefield now—guests screaming, glass shattering, gunfire echoing against the vaulted ceilings.

I know she's looking for her husband, but mine is bleeding out on the floor. "We need to get to Leon."

His sister pales and nods quickly, leading us forward, cutting through the crowds as fast as possible. Her movements are desperate as we inch closer to where Leon fell.

I just have enough wherewithal to notice an attack to the

right of us. I launch myself to block the knife that would have embedded itself in Isabella's shoulder and yank back his arm hard enough for bones to snap.

Isabella twirls in alarm and immediately goes for the two men behind him, taking one down before they even have a chance to strike.

Cassandra—never one to be outdone—swings her bottle haphazardly at the other, the jagged edge catching his arm.

He curses and stumbles back, giving me enough time to drive my heel into his knee.

I can't wait to see if he goes down. I'm already spinning back to my original course. Through the throngs of bodies, I catch glimpses of him on the ground. Someone is leaning over him.

Someone is there already. Someone is already saving him. Please. Please. Please.

Just as it feels like we're finally making progress, another wave of bodies crashes into us.

I reach for Isabella, but she's swept away in the surge, dragging Cas with her.

"Mia!" Isabella's voice is already distant.

I don't have a choice. I can't spare the time to follow them, not now. I have to get to him. I won't stop. Not until I reach him.

I fight my way through the crowd, but it's so much harder now that I'm doing it alone. Why was he so far away? Why had I let him go?

Every step feels like I'm being dragged deeper into a nightmare. The floor feels slick underfoot, and I'm dizzy from the ring of gunfire and a scream that I think is coming from me.

Then suddenly, I'm yanked backward out of the fray.

Unfamiliar hands roughly pull me to one side. My breath catches in my throat, and I spin, lashing out.

My fist connects with someone's jaw with a satisfying crunch. But I can't celebrate before another set of hands snatches at my wrists, pinning them behind my back.

Two men wrestle me into submission as I fight for my life. I'm thrashing and struggling in a way I never knew I was capable of as my arms are bound tight.

The sharp pressure of an arm around my neck forces the air from my lungs, and I fight against the suffocating grip. I twist, trying to break free, but my strength is slipping away, the black spots creeping into my vision.

And then, just as I think I can't take it anymore—when the fight starts to drain from me—I hear a voice.

"Mia!"

The voice is familiar, the deep rumble of it something I've heard countless times before. I thrash against my restraints so that I can see my savior approaching.

"Max," I gasp, my chest heaving. "Help!"

But the man approaches slowly, unhurried by the situation. At first, I thought he might be weighing up my would-be-kidnappers. But they don't go for him either.

Instead, he leans over me, a curious expression on his face. "You're a hard woman to kidnap, Mrs. Natali."

The shock of his words is undermined by the pure adrenaline running through my veins. "Who the fuck do you think you are? Let me go!"

He pulls something from his pocket. I brace for a knife, but it's something altogether more sinister. A syringe.

"The kind of man who isn't going to take any chances

with a firecracker like you," he says as he flicks the thin, glass tool and levels it to my neck.

I try to squirm away, but it's no use. There are two sets of hands holding me still when a third shoves the needle under my skin and plunges its contents into my bloodstream.

He has the audacity to look smug as he steps away. The world around us is already distorting and fading behind him.

"The Cartel don't keep prisoners for long. I'm sure you'll be reunited with your dear husband soon."

Max's voice is the last thing I hear.

The blackness pulls me under, and I can't fight it anymore. My last thought is of Leon—praying to whatever gods will listen that he's still alive.

My head throbs as I wake up, a dull, persistent ache that bleeds into my thoughts.

It takes a few moments for my mind to catch up, for the haze of unconsciousness to lift enough for me to recognize my surroundings. Cold stone walls. A dim light overhead. The metallic smell of rust in the air.

I inhale sharply, panic rising like a tidal wave in my chest.

I'm in a holding cell.

My wrists are bound tightly to the arms of a chair, the rough ropes biting into my skin. My body aches—head, shoulders, and stomach—they're all sore like I've been dragged across the earth.

Every instinct screams at me to move, to escape, but I can't. My limbs feel heavy, sluggish, trapped, likely a side effect of whatever they drugged me with back at the...

And then, it hits me.

Leon.

My breath catches in my throat, and my heart drops. I can barely force the thought through my mind—*is he alive?*

I remember his body crumpling, blood spreading across the casino floor.

No.

I force the thought away, pushing it down, unwilling to believe it. I can't think like that. I can't. He's not gone. He can't be.

Tears well in my eyes, but I refuse to let them fall. Not now. I need to think up a plan to get out of here.

The ropes bite into my skin as I shift in my chair, trying to find an angle of weakness. But whoever tied me up knew exactly what they were doing.

Nausea curls in my stomach. Max. Had Max done this?

Oh, I'm going to fucking kill him. Slowly, painfully. The way he deserves, that traitor.

Minutes pass, or hours—I can't tell. Time stretches, a dull blur of waiting, my body stiffening with every passing second as I attempt everything I can think of to free myself.

I let my anger fuel me through it. It's easier than the terror of what I saw, of the possibility that he might not be...

Just as the weight of those thoughts feels too much to bear, the door to the cell creaks open. My heart skips, and I snap my head toward the sound, hoping—*praying*—it's Leon.

But it isn't.

I feel the dread settle into my bones as her dark features turn on me. As emotionless and cold as the last time I saw her.

Carmen.

The Cartel Princess.

26

LEON

I wake with a sharp inhale, like I've been ripped out of a nightmare and hurled into a world of pain.

The ache in my chest is instant and excruciating like someone's sitting on my ribs, pressing down with unbearable weight. My head spins as I blink up at the sterile white ceiling, the smell of antiseptic flooding my nose.

It takes me a second to piece it all together—where I am, why my body feels like it's been smashed to pieces. But then it comes rushing back in a wave of red-hot fury and agonizing dread.

Max.

The gunshot.

Mia.

My pulse spikes, echoed by a nearby heart monitor.

I need to move, to find her, to protect her. But when I try to sit up, pain rips through me like a lightning bolt, forcing me back down with a groan.

"Easy there, Leon," Isabella's voice cuts through the panic, hoarse but familiar.

I turn my head, finding her sitting in a chair by the bed. She looks like she hasn't slept in days, dressed in a hoodie that definitely doesn't belong to her.

"Where's Mia?"

My sister's eyes scan my face, my body—lingering on my chest—before she sighs and pinches the bridge of her nose in a gesture that's so reminiscent of Teo I almost do a double-take.

"Safe," Isabella says quickly, firmly. "She wasn't hurt in the attack."

I stare at her hunched form momentarily as I roll her words through my mind. Trying to decide if it's enough to offer me some relief.

It's not

"Where is she?" I try again.

Isabella hesitates. It's a small moment, one that I doubt anyone else would notice unless they'd known her from birth.

But before she can answer, the door opens, and a doctor walks in—a middle-aged man with sharp eyes,

"You're awake," he says, glancing at a clipboard before looking at me. "That's a good start."

"What happened?" I growl, frustration bubbling over.

"You were incredibly lucky," the doctor says, setting the clipboard down.

"The bullet hit your chest, but it struck a rib at an angle, deflecting it away from your heart and major arteries. It punctured a lung, but we were able to stabilize you quickly enough to prevent permanent damage. You underwent surgery to repair the lung and stop the bleeding."

I exhale sharply, trying to process his words. The

memory of the shot, the staggering blow to the chest, flashes through my mind.

I clench my fists to ward off the memory. "How long have I been out?"

"Three days," Isabella says quietly. "We've been taking shifts watching over you."

"Three days," I mutter, the weight of it settling on my bruising chest. "And Mia?"

"She's alive," Isabella says, starting to sound irritated. "I told you this."

I narrow my eyes at her. "No, you said she was safe."

"Isn't that the same thing?"

The doctor clears his throat. "You need to rest, Mr. Moretti. Your body's been through a major trauma, and pushing yourself too soon could cause complications. The lung will take weeks to fully heal."

I barely hear him, too busy staring down my sister. "Isabella."

She doesn't look at me; her chin points up stubbornly. "You almost died, Leon. We thought...I thought..."

"Issy. Look at me."

When she does, there are tears in her eyes. "I'm sorry, Leon."

My mind is already racing, calculating, planning. Already jumping to every worst possible conclusion before she has a chance to draw another breath and speak out the last words I want to hear.

"They took her. The Cartel took her."

For a moment, I let the words wash over me, feeling an eerie kind of calm settle into my bones. Then, the world narrows to a singular focus: Mia.

I shove the blanket off me and swing my legs over the

side of the bed, ignoring the fire burning in my chest. My breath hitches, but I grit my teeth against the pain. Every second wasted here is a second Mia is at their mercy.

"Sir, please don't—" the doctor tries.

"Leon, stop!" Isabella begs.

"She's out there, Isabella. I'm not going to sit here and do nothing," I roar as the room tilts violently, my knees buckling under me.

Before I can hit the ground, the door slams open, and Dante storms in, followed by Teo. Dante's face is tight with worry as he slides himself under my arm and hoists me back up.

But Teo's expression is stone cold, his eyes seemingly entirely black as they lock on me like a predator about to pounce.

"Sit down," Teo orders, his voice like a whip.

"I'm not staying here." I shrug away from Dante, gripping the edge of the bed to steady myself. "Mia needs me."

"She needs you alive, Leon," Teo retorts, crossing the room in three long strides.

He grabs my arm and shoves me back onto the bed with more force than necessary. There's no mistaking the ruthless don in his dominance, and I instinctively snarl and push back. But his hands are too firm, his jaw tight as he holds me there.

"You're no good to her dead. You are no good to *me* dead. We need everyone right now, and you will NOT lose your head over this."

I narrow my eyes at him, ready to rip out his damn throat if I need to.

"Enough!" she snaps, her voice slicing through the

tension. "Leon, calm the fuck down. You're acting deranged. This is exactly why I didn't want to tell you."

"You lied to me."

"I lie to you *all the time,* dingus," Issy groans. "Snap out of it. We need you firing on all cylinders here, not throwing yourself on a suicide mission trying to climb a flight of stairs, all right?"

No one speaks to me like Issy. No one has ever had the death wish, honestly. Yet it's her words that temper the near-endless pit of rage that has consumed me since the moment I found out Mia was missing.

Sensing the shift in mood, Dante takes a bold step closer. "Leon, listen. You need to know what happened at the casino."

I close my eyes, grit my teeth, and exhale. "Tell me."

Everyone around me visibly relaxes. The doctor coughs awkwardly and makes his escape. Dante starts speaking once the door is firmly closed.

"It was chaos after Max shot you. He wasn't working alone. The Cartel had servers planted as operatives. They were waiting for his signal. As soon as you hit the ground, they went straight for her."

He steps closer, as if he can block my escape if I try again to race out of the room.

"Mia fought like hell," Dante continues, his voice softening. "She was holding her own until they overwhelmed her. I saw them dragging her out just as reinforcements arrived. By the time we pushed the Cartel back, they were gone. Max included."

"Max..." I growl, the betrayal cutting deeper than the bullet ever could.

"We tracked him all the way back to a compound in

Long Island. That's where all of Rubio's forces seem to be regrouping," Teo says. "But we have other problems, Leon."

I fix my gaze on him, already dreading his next words. "Spit it out."

"Max didn't just betray us by aligning with the Cartel," Teo begins, his voice grim. "He's been feeding us lies for months, severely inflating the damage we've done to Amos Rubio's network. The Cartel isn't as weak as we thought."

I let his words sink in, a slow burn of rage building in my chest. "How badly did he twist it?"

"Badly," Teo says bluntly. "All those supply lines Dante thought we'd taken out? Most are still running. The smuggling routes we thought were torched? Fully operational."

Dante runs a hand down his face, the realization hitting him just as hard. "That son of a bitch."

"And it gets worse," Teo cuts in, his voice tightening. "The attack at the casino was just the beginning. Max coordinated simultaneous strikes on both of our families—the Guild and the Prince's Hand."

I'm going to murder that traitorous bastard with my bare hands.

"My warehouses were hit last night, and my men are still fighting to take them back. Four of your casinos in Manhattan were robbed mercilessly. We've both been crippled."

I grip the edge of the bed, my knuckles whitening.

"Rubio's playing this perfectly," I mutter. "And I let his crown jester into my fucking court."

"No one is blaming you, Leon." Isabella's voice is softer than the others, but it doesn't take the sting away.

Teo leans back, his eyes sharp and calculating. "But we

need to be smart about this right now. We regroup, dig in, focus on recovery—"

"No."

His dark eyes flash with surprise.

"We don't dig in. We don't wait." I sit up straighter, ignoring the stabbing pain in my chest. "We hit Amos Rubio where it hurts. Now. Before he can consolidate his gains."

"You're serious," Dante says, arching a brow.

"Dead serious," I snap. "Rubio thinks he's crippled us, which means he's overconfident. He'll be celebrating his victory, holed up in that mansion of his. If we wait, he'll regroup and come for us again, this time with everything he's got."

Teo shakes his head. "We're spread thin, Leon. We've got manpower issues, supply issues. And let's not forget you just got shot."

I glare at him. "Rubio took my wife. I'm not giving him time to gloat."

"You're thinking emotionally," Teo counters, his voice low and steady. "This isn't just about Mia. It's about the survival of the entire Italian empire in New York. You can't throw what's left of us at him without a plan."

"You think I don't have a plan? I've been playing chess with Amos Rubio for months. I know his weaknesses."

Teo exchanges a glance with Dante, then sighs. "Fine. Let's hear it."

"We go straight for Rubio's compound," I say. "The heart of his operation. We catch him off guard, make him bleed, and make it clear that we're still standing."

"It's risky," Dante says, rubbing his jaw.

"It's necessary," I reply. "Gather what we have left. I'll lead the attack myself."

"No, you won't," Teo says flatly. "You're not leaving this bed until you're cleared to stand without toppling over. If you insist on moving forward with this, fine. But Dante and I are running point."

I want to argue, but I know he's not backing down. Not here, not now. Hell, my own body is screaming at me to stay down, to heal.

But Isabella isn't the only one who knows how to lie.

"Fine. But you take my plan at my word," I say, leaning back with a grim smile. "You'd better burn that mansion to the ground."

Dante nods, his eyes cold. "It'll be ashes by sunrise."

27

MIA

You would have thought by now that I might have become well acquainted with imprisonment. Perhaps, on some masochistic level, my isolated pregnancy had almost prepared me for this.

But I would do it again—nine months of loneliness. I'd do it a hundred times to spare myself three days of agony.

Three days of confinement, fear, and a silence so thick I can barely breathe through it.

When I close my eyes, I try to picture Liza and Luca's tiny faces, the way their small hands grasped at mine. The thought of them makes my chest ache and my spirits soar. Do they miss me? Will they even remember me if I don't make it out of here?

And Leon...

Is he dead? Is he dead? Is he dead?

The words echo through me more consistently than my one heartbeat.

"She doesn't shut up, even in her sleep," someone sneers.

Another chuckles—a low and ugly sound. "She'll crack soon enough. They always do."

My stomach growls a loud and empty protest. I've barely eaten since they dragged me here, and I'm not sure I could keep food down even if I had it. I bite down hard on my lip, forcing myself not to react.

Let them think I'm breaking. Let them underestimate me.

My cell is a windowless box barely big enough to stand in. The cot I lie in smells of mildew, but it's better than the cold floor.

Sleep doesn't come. I'm constantly haunted by the fractured memories of Leon bleeding on the casino floor and the twins crying out for me. I thrash against the blankets, jolting into a state of half-consciousness as I try to reach for them.

I swallow hard, a fresh wave of tears threatening to spill. I can't let myself think like this. Not when the guards outside are looking for any excuse to make my life a misery.

Like every other day, time passes until the moment the cell door opens.

The guards aren't gentle. They learned the hard way that I'm not some subdued little damsel in distress—the scabbed-over scratch marks on their faces are a testament to that.

My body is a live wire of exhaustion, every muscle trembling as I shuffle down the dim hallway, guards flanking me on either side. Their hands hover near their weapons, just in case.

From what I've managed to deduce so far, I'm in some kind of compound. I've been stealing glances as we walk down corridors that seem alive with activity.

It's sprawling, like an ant colony, with corridors branching off into who-knows-where. I count every door, every intersection, every detail I can store away for later—if later ever comes.

But there are too many of them. Everywhere I look, eyes follow me, sizing me up. Waiting for me to step out of line.

The interrogation room is stark and cold; its single metal chair bolted to the floor before a table. The guards waste no time tying me up, my restraints biting into my skin as I sink into the unforgiving seat.

The fluorescent light overhead buzzes faintly, a persistent hum that drills into my skull. The room feels smaller today, or maybe it's just me shrinking under the weight of exhaustion and hunger.

Just like every other day, Carmen enters a bit later.

Her posture is perfect, hands folded neatly on the table. Her beautiful curls are tied back from her blank face, making her usually soft features seem so much more severe. Or perhaps that's just the lighting.

"Tell me where they're moving next, Mia." Her voice is a razor slicing through the silence.

Perhaps it's just the lighting, but there's torment in her expression, in the darkness of her eyes, the bags beneath them, the tightness of her lips, the bob of her throat. A slight tremor in her hand.

Oh Carmen, what did they do to you?

"You already know the answer to that." I hold her gaze, my throat dry, my voice scratchy from disuse.

"Tell me where Teo Vitale is hiding."

"I don't know," I bite out.

Round and round in circles, all over again.

"You're aware of what my father is capable of?" her cold

tone betrays a hint of irritation. "You're aware of what happens to you if you don't cooperate?"

I stick out my chin stubbornly. "I'd rather die."

Her eyes narrow, furious flames cracking through the ice. "When did you learn to be so loyal?"

And there it is. The crux of it all.

Beneath the months of grief and isolation and torment lies the huge emotion that started it all: guilt.

I betrayed Carmen Rubio, and I would do it again if it kept my family safe. But there's not one second that I don't regret throwing her back into that world without so much as a tether to reality.

I saw firsthand how they treated her and knew they intended so much worse for the debutant, and yet I walked away with the belief that I never once cared for her.

The truth is that I did, more so than I had ever intended. I still do.

"You don't need to do this, Carmen," I whisper.

Her gaze hardens, and she leans back in her chair. "What I need is for you to answer these damn questions so he doesn't kill you."

"Why are you doing this? You don't have to follow him—be like him. You're better than this."

For the first time, her composure completely cracks.

"Better?" she spits, her voice trembling with barely contained anger. "I trusted you, Mia. I thought you cared about me. But the whole time, you were lying. Spying. Using me."

Her words hit me like a punch to the gut. "Carmen—"

"Don't!" she cuts me off, her voice rising. Her eyes glisten, but she blinks rapidly, refusing to let the tears fall.

"You're smarter than this, Mia. Make yourself invaluable, please. Give me something. Please."

My heart begins to break. "You shouldn't care about that."

"You think I don't know that? When you turned out exactly like everyone else? Playing me. Manipulating me."

"I care about you too," I whisper, the words barely audible.

She slams her hand down on the table, making me flinch. "No, you don't! If you cared, you wouldn't have betrayed me."

I can't answer that. I don't know how to. The silence stretches between us, thick and suffocating.

Carmen wipes a hand across her face, her jaw tight as she fights to regain control.

"You were the only person I thought was real," she murmurs, more to herself than to me. "And now you're just...nothing but a walking death wish."

She rises from her chair abruptly, pushing it back with a screech. For a moment, I think she's going to storm out, but she pauses at the door, her back to me.

"Tell me why, Mia," she says quietly. "Why did you do it?"

I open my mouth, the words forming on my tongue, but the sudden wail of an alarm cut me off.

The shrill, piercing sound makes me jump, and I see Carmen flinch, too, her hand jerking back from the door as if it were electrified.

My heart hammers in my chest, a wild hope blooming inside me despite my better judgment. If that alarm is what I think it is...

"No." Carmen's wide, panicked eyes meet mine. For a

fleeting moment, she's just a young woman caught in the crossfire of something far bigger than herself.

"They're here, aren't they?" It comes out like I'm begging her to confirm it.

She takes a shaking step away from the door. "They'll kill me."

"No, Carmen, listen to me," I say, leaning forward as much as my restraints allow. "I won't let that happen. You just need to let me go."

She's already shaking her head like she can't process what I'm saying. "No. I can't. My father—"

"Your father isn't here, is he?" It's a shot in the dark, but why else would she look so terrified? "No one else is here to protect you. Please, let me do it again, one last time."

Her lips tremble, hesitating as the alarm shrieks through the room.

I press on, desperate. "Please. You trusted me once. Trust me now. Let me go."

Her jaw clenches, tears glistening in her eyes. For a moment, I think she will walk away, to leave us both to our wretched fates.

But then, with a sharp inhale, she takes a decisive step toward me.

The door bursts open, and both of us freeze.

28

LEON

The chaos outside the compound is deafening: gunfire cracks through the air, punctuated by the occasional explosion that rattles the earth beneath my feet. Smoke curls into the night sky, blotting out the stars.

It's a damn symphony of war, and I should be directing it, not skulking in the shadows like a ghost.

But Mia is inside. And that's all that matters.

The hardest part had been convincing Teo that I intended to stay and commit to my bed rest. Slipping out of the hospital had been child's play.

I press my back to the concrete wall of the perimeter, the coarse surface biting into my shoulder blades. Every step I take sends a fiery ache through me, radiating outward from the bullet wound in my chest.

I'm slower than I'd like to be, stiffer to avoid agitating the wound that is packed under enough gauze that I may as well be wearing a corset. But I use the pain to sharpen my instincts as I peer around the corner of the wall.

What remains of the Guild and the Prince's Hand have swarmed the compound. They're focused on the main entrance, drawing the Cartel's fire.

Amos Rubio's men are pouring out like ants from a hill, armed to the teeth. The Guild's tech specialists hacked into the compound's surveillance system, leaving the enemy blind to anything but what's in front of them.

Which serves my purposes perfectly.

I slip through a side entrance, a rusted maintenance door I remember from the blueprints. It's unguarded—likely overlooked in the chaos—and creaks like a dying animal when I push it open. The sound makes me grit my teeth.

The hallway beyond is dimly lit, the faint hum of fluorescent lights overhead barely cutting through the darkness. The muffled sounds of battle grow distant as I venture deeper.

I stick close to the wall, my steps careful, my breathing controlled. My reactions are slower, my movements less precise. But my ears prickle at every sound, and my eyes are sharp and alert.

I'm still a weapon of war.

The first man I encounter rounds a corner without checking his angles. Sloppy.

I'm on him before he can react, my hand clamping over his mouth while my blade finds the soft flesh between his ribs. His muffled scream is short-lived, his body sagging into my arms as I lower him to the ground silently.

I wipe the blood on his uniform and keep moving, my chest burning with every step.

I check the next corner to find two guards stationed at

the end of the corridor, blocking my path. I press myself into the shadows, fingers curling around the hilt of my knife.

My chest burns in protest as I breathe deeply. Every movement needs to count.

When one of them turns away to adjust his earpiece, I strike. A single, brutal slash to the first man's throat before he can blink.

The second guard raises his weapon, but I'm already inside his range, driving the knife into his gut and twisting until he falls silent.

The hallway is clear again, but my breath comes heavier now, the pain in my chest a roaring fire. I collapse to my knees, darkness threatening to encompass my vision.

"Fuck," I breathe, and I breathe, half-heartedly backing up against the wall in case someone charges through the doors.

If anyone finds me here, vulnerable and exposed like this…

I don't think about it. I think about Mia. Mia is here. Liza and Luca are waiting with Isabella for her. They need their mother.

I need my wife.

The roaring flames in my chest begin to subside, and I shakily break open the painkillers I brought in case of emergency. They'll make me more sluggish, but I can't collapse like this again.

Not when Max is somewhere in this hellhole.

I slowly get to my feet and return to my mission.

The air grows heavier as I move deeper into the compound, the smell of gunpowder mixing with the acrid stench of blood.

The fight seems both inches away and too far out of

reach. Every time I think it's getting closer, I turn another corner, and it's faded back again.

The blueprints indicated that the cell block was near a wide storage room on the ground floor. It was perhaps presumptuous of me to think that such a non-vital space would be left unguarded and that the bigger threat would be stationed outside the prison.

This much becomes clear as I slip into the storage room, only to be greeted by a slow clap, halting me in my tracks.

Max.

He stands in a wide storage room, leaning casually against a stack of crates as if this is all some kind of joke. A pistol dangles loosely from his hand, his gaze sharp and his smile threatening as he surveys the state I'm in.

"I gotta say, Leon. You're one hard man to kill," he says, straightening slightly.

This is the man I trusted for months. The mastermind behind my every downfall.

"What can I say? You're a sloppy shot." I twirl the knife in my fingers as I stalk toward him.

Max's smile only widens. He steps forward, closing the gap between us.

I can see the confidence in his eyes—the kind of arrogance that comes from knowing you've got the upper hand.

"You look like hell, boss," he taunts, gesturing to my chest. "That little souvenir I gave you slowing you down? You should've stayed in your hospital bed."

I lunge at him, slashing low with my knife, but he's ready. He sidesteps, the blade missing his gut by a fraction of an inch. His fist connects with my ribs, and pain explodes through my torso, nearly driving me to my knees.

"See? You're too slow now. Too weak," he circles me like

a predator. "Is Teo Vitale so desperate that he'd send an invalid to do his dirty work?"

He kicks my knife from my hand, sending it skittering across the floor. I barely dodge the next blow, using his momentum to drive my shoulder into his chest.

He staggers back with a laugh. "No, that's not his style, is it? You're here on your own. Couldn't resist the temptation to play the hero, could you?"

I freeze as Max levels his gun on me, a damning sense of deja-vu hammering through my burning chest.

"What's that little wife of yours going to think when I tell her you were too weak to save her?"

The fire is unbearable. The pain is intolerable. I close my eyes and breathe, praying that my legs will hold out.

I'm a fast draw, but with Max's gun already pointed at my chest...

"You're pathetic, Leon. I hope you die knowing it was all for nothing."

My legs give out.

Bang.

The bullet soars over my head, where my torso had been a fraction of a second before.

I don't think. I just draw.

The angle is terrible, and I'm unable to compensate entirely for my body's awkward trajectory. But the trigger is pulled just before I black out from the pain of hitting the floor.

I wake up several seconds later, wishing I were dead. There's blood seeping into my shirt from where my wound is leaking. I'm out of time.

But there's something else. A choking noise only a few feet away.

With the remainder of my strength, I turn my head to find Max stumbling to his knees, hands clutched to his throat.

The bullet had shot clean through it.

His eyes are wide with shock as he collapses into a pool of his own blood.

It's done.

I close my eyes and go back to sleep.

Hours pass. Minutes. Seconds. I can't be sure. Nothing has any meaning but the brutal pain in my chest and the dizzy, spinning that keeps me pressed to the floor.

"LEON!" Dante's voice cuts through my unconsciousness with the brutality of a gong.

My eyes snap open to the sight of him crowding over me; medical kit splayed open at my side. Vaguely, I'm aware that my shirt has been removed, and my chest feels tighter again.

"YOU STUPID BASTARD!"

"Maybe," I concede with a groan as I prop myself up on my elbows. "But I shot Max in the throat."

"You could have died!" He throws his hands up in the air in exasperation.

"I didn't. I'm fine."

"The hell you are," he growls as he helps me to my feet. "We're leaving. Now."

"I'm going to the cell block. You can't stop me," I snap.

Dante groans, pinching the bridge of his nose like I'm the world's biggest headache. "Teo will fucking kill me if I don't get you out of here."

"Then get me out of here...let's just leave via the cell block," I challenge, meeting his gaze. "It's just over here."

He exhales sharply, shaking his head. "You're insane."

I know the fight has left him as I slap him on the

shoulder while making my way to the double doors on the far side of the room.

Dante is at my side in an instant, pushing past us to deal with the door guards stationed behind it.

"This must be it," he mutters as we take in the long corridor and the door to the left where the guards had been posted.

I don't hesitate to kick it down, bursting into the room with my gun raised.

But it's not breathtaking green eyes that stare down the barrel. It's brown one. Eyes I never thought I'd see here.

29

MIA

It's a ghost.

It's a wrathful God.

And he's pointing a gun at Carmen's face.

"Leon!" I cry, my voice breaking.

Leon is there, shirtless and blood-stained, and his chest rises and falls with every labored breath. His eyes lock on me instantly, and for a moment, the entire world narrows down to just us.

He's alive. He's alive. He's here. He came for me.

A sob wrecks itself through my body.

In my periphery, Carmen flinches at the sound.

Leon immediately turns back to the woman before him, his face set in ruthless determination.

"NO!" I half scream. I pant in desperate relief as his finger falls from the trigger. "Don't hurt her."

He doesn't drop the gun, doesn't look away from her. "Are you all right, Mia?"

"You're alive. God, you're alive."

"Mia," he barks, and Carmen takes a trembling step back.

"I'm okay. Leon, leave her alone. She has nothing to do with this."

I watch as Leon considers my words, eyes narrowing as he scans the threat before him. Then, with a small gesture with his gun, he says, "Untie her."

Carmen swallows but does not reply. She's clearly gathering her nerve to turn away from the gun to approach me slowly. I can see the terror in her eyes—she's too young to be shaped by this world as of yet.

She should be out there using her degree to do something that excites her, living a real life, changing the world.

She shouldn't be here.

"Hey," I say to her softly. "It's okay. He's not going to shoot you."

"Mia," his voice is a warning.

"He's not," I snap at him. "He's going to put the fucking gun down."

Carmen trembles as she steps behind me. I can feel it in her hands as she unties my bindings.

Leon stands before us, and I stare at him defiantly until he drops his gun. At his shoulder, I see the unmistakable outline of Dante crowding the doorframe.

"I'm sorry," I whisper to Carmen.

She says nothing, but the bindings drop, and I sigh in relief. I turn to her immediately, wanting to reach out and comfort her, but she's already retreated into the corner of the room.

"Get out," she whispers.

I back away, reaching out behind me for Leon. His hand

immediately finds mine and pulls insistently. Tugging me out of the room.

Dante hesitates by the door to give Carmen a casual salute. "Princess." Before slamming it closed behind us.

Leon's arms are around me in a second, pulling me into his chest as hands cradle my face like I'm something sacred.

And oh, oh. He's alive. His deep, chocolate eyes bore into mine with the intensity of a man deprived of the sight.

I feel another sob building in my chest, but he kisses it back. His lips are warm and alive on mine.

Alive and alive and alive.

"Mia," he murmurs, his voice thick with emotion. His hands tremble as they slide over my back and my arms, as though he's trying to convince himself I'm real.

"I thought—" I half choke on the words as he kisses up my cheeks and across my nose. "I thought you were dead."

Next to us, Dante clears his throat. "He might be if we don't get you both out of here right now."

Leon's jaw tightens, but he nods, gripping my hand tightly as he pulls away toward the exit. With Dante close on our heels, he pushes open the double doors into some kind of storage room.

Only to freeze when he sees who's waiting on the other side.

"You bastard."

Teo Vitale stands up from where he was crouched over the body of...oh...

Behind him, Rocco barks orders at the men who are filing in behind. "I need a B team to escort these guys out immediately!"

But Leon's focus is on the other don. "I had to get her out."

"I told you to stay in the hospital!" Teo snaps, striding toward us. "Look at you. You're about to collapse."

Leon stiffens, and for the first time I notice how awkwardly he's holding himself and just how labored his breathing is. Out of the harsh lighting of the interrogation room, his skin is pale and gray.

"What the hell did you do to yourself?" I hiss at him, but he shrugs me off.

"Get out of here now. Rocco's team will escort you out," Teo orders before he turns to me. "It's good to see you, Mia, but please, take this man home. I don't want to see his face for another month."

I give my husband a long look. "Let's make it two. Come on, let's go."

His shoulders slump, and he nods, defeated.

I don't comment as he leans into me as we make our escape. Dante and Rocco are on either side as we push out of the compound.

The hallways are a labyrinth of chaos. Gunfire, shouting, and the acrid smell of smoke fill the air. Leon keeps me close, shielding me with his body as we weave through the wreckage.

By the time we make it outside, I'm gasping for breath, and the man at my side is becoming a dead weight. It takes all three of us to get him into a car, and my arms barely feel strong enough to grip the wheel as I sit in the driver's seat.

I manage to turn on the ignition, only to find myself hesitating. "Where am I going?"

Despite how pale and broken he looks, Leon cracks a small smile. "Home."

∽

When I finally pull up to the brownstone, I almost don't recognize it.

The last time I saw it, the building was charred and broken. But now, it looks pristine—rebuilt and restored with painstaking attention to detail. The front steps gleam welcomingly under the streetlights, the door is inviting and warm.

A sob catches in my throat as I stare at it, tears burning my eyes. I wasn't sure I'd ever see it again.

"You fixed it," I murmur as we come to a stop just outside.

His lips twitch into the ghost of a smile. "Wanted...you to have it back."

I get out and rush to Leon's side of the car, helping him out with one arm around his waist.

Inside, the air smells faintly of paint and wood polish, but the layout is the same. I help him up the stairs, practically dragging him into his room. He collapses onto the bed with a groan, completely drenched in sweat.

With a start, I realize he's bleeding through his bandages again. I immediately turn to grab the medical supplies, but his hands snatch at my wrist.

"Don't go."

"I'll be back in a moment," I squeeze his arm gently. "I won't leave, I promise."

With that, I race down the stairs, feeling lightheaded when I arrive in the kitchen. Right. Food. Starving for three days.

I inhale a banana and down a glass of water while searching for the medical kit, finally spying it tucked behind the sink. I run back upstairs.

Leon has his eyes closed when I arrive, and my heart surges at the sight of his prone body.

"I'm back, Leon. I'm going to look after you, okay?" My voice catches, but thankfully, he stirs at the sound.

My hands shake as I peel back his bloodied bandages, revealing the splitting stitches across his chest. The sight of it nearly sends me spiraling again, but I force myself to focus.

"Just breathe, Leon. I've got you," I say, dabbing at the wound with antiseptic. "But this is going to hurt."

I rummage around for a suture needle, but there's no anesthetic to be found. I contemplate raiding his supply of whiskey.

"Just do it," he grits out, his eyes half-lidded. "Now."

I thread the needle, trying to ignore how clammy his skin feels under my touch. The first pass through the torn flesh makes him jerk, his breath hissing through his teeth.

"Leon, look at me," I say softly, leaning closer. "Do you remember the first time we met?"

His eyes flick to mine, hazy with pain, but he nods.

"You were threatening Teo over something stupid," I say, pulling the thread through again. "I thought, 'this man is far too attractive to have more than a couple of brain cells spare'."

A faint smirk touches his lips despite the sweat beading on his brow. "You were...infuriating," he murmurs.

"And you were smarter than you looked," I reply, my voice trembling slightly as I work on the next stitch. "I've always...liked that about you. Even when I shouldn't have."

His hand weakly grasps mine, his fingers tightening as I push the needle through another torn edge.

"Keep talking," he says, his voice a raw whisper.

I do, recounting little moments—our arguments, impassioned kisses, the first time we held the twins together.

His breathing steadies, though his grip on my hand remains firm like I'm his tether to something beyond the pain.

At last, I tie off the thread, sitting back with a shaky exhale.

"Done," I whisper, brushing a hand through his damp hair.

Leon's gaze is heavy, full of something I can't quite name. "You're...incredible."

My throat tightens as his eyes flutter closed. His breathing immediately slows into unconsciousness.

I watch him for a moment, entirely overwhelmed by the last few days, before sinking into bed next to him. Everything else can wait a while.

"I love you too."

30

LEON

The days blur together, a haze of pain, exhaustion, and fleeting lucidity. I drift in and out of consciousness, the world around me reduced to fragments of sensation and sound.

Mia is the constant in the haze. Her warmth is always by my side at night, her hands fussing with blankets, smoothing over my forehead, or checking my bandages.

Sometimes, I wake to the sound of her humming softly, the melody tugging at some buried corner of my heart. Other times, I catch the edge of her whispered words—half-lovely, half-threatening.

Never those same words I heard through the exhaustion that first night.

When I'm awake long enough to speak, I try to reassure her, but the effort always drains me.

"I'm...fine," I manage once, my voice barely above a rasp.

She glares at me, her eyes red-rimmed but fierce. "What you are is stubborn. Go back to sleep."

But her harshness is always mellowed by her touches: a soft press of her hand on mine, a gentle kiss on my forehead.

Then, one day, the haze clears enough for a singular moment of clarity. I wake to a tiny weight being placed in my arms.

"Easy," Mia whispers, guiding my hands. I look down and see our daughter, Liza. Her little fists wave in the air, her eyes squinting up at me, and for a second, I can't breathe.

"She's beautiful," I manage, my voice cracking. Mia smiles, though her eyes shimmer with tears.

"And here's her brother," she says, placing Luca in the crook of my other arm.

My chest tightens—not with pain this time, but with something deeper, something anchoring.

"Your Aunty Isabella has been taking such good care of you, hasn't she?" Mia coos at them both. "I'll put them to bed soon. I just wanted them to say hello."

"It's good to have them both back," I breathe.

Mia's expression softens. "Our family is back together again."

As the weeks pass, the fog of pain and countering medicines lifts. But my mobility remains limited.

Mia doesn't let me wallow, not even for a second.

"If you're strong enough to argue, you're strong enough to heal," she says one day, propping pillows behind me.

I stroke along her arm absently as she does, but she snatches it away quickly, shooting me a dark glare. "No. Not again. You are *resting*, Leon."

"I've missed you." The words are so devastatingly true, I think for a moment I see her resolve weakening.

It doesn't last. "You should have thought about that before you came to rescue me with a hole in your chest."

Dante visits one quiet afternoon, his carefree smile easier than I've seen it in months as he leans through my bedroom door. From the glances he keeps chucking out into the hallway, I doubt he's supposed to be here.

"The Cartel's licking their wounds," he says hurriedly. "A ceasefire's in place. Tentative, but there's been no pushback. Both sides need time to recover."

"Not for long. Amos will be planning something."

"Of course. But for now, rest. We'll need you at full strength when this peace inevitably falls apart." Dante smirks before leaning in, conspiring. "And between you and me, Teo doesn't have the knack for war that you do."

I chuckle to myself. "Careful, Dante, that sounds like slander."

"I'm just telling it like it is." Dante shrugs. "Teo knows I've always been a free spirit."

"Well, if you fancy a career upgrade, I need a new second."

Before Dante can respond, Mia comes in behind him, carrying a sleeping Luca. She gives him a look that could wither steel.

"I thought I told you to leave him alone. He's resting," she says firmly, setting our son in one of the matching bassinets that now inhabit the corner of my room.

Dante raises his hands in surrender but winks at me before leaving.

It's late in the evening when I wake up to the sound of music coming from downstairs.

Now that I can use the gym again, my mobility is

improving nicely. I even managed to shower after my last workout without wincing under the hot stream of water.

Healing is never linear, but when I come to with the sweet melody in my ears, I swear I've never felt better.

Quietly, I throw on a shirt and pad down the stairs to investigate. I stop in the doorway to the living room, and my breath catches.

Mia is there, swaying gracefully in the center of the room. Her long, wavy red hair cascades down her back, catching the light like a halo of fire. She's wearing one of my shirts, oversized on her frame, the sleeves rolled up as she twirls gently.

Luca is nestled close in her arms, his tiny head resting against her shoulder. Beside her, Liza dozes in her bassinet, already fast asleep.

I lean against the doorframe, unable to look away. Mia's green eyes are bright, focused entirely on the twins. She hums along to the song as if the world beyond these walls doesn't exist.

I'm not sure how long I stand there, just watching her. Admiring her.

In this moment, she is everything—strength, beauty, love. The thought pierces through me: I don't deserve her. Not after everything I've put her through. And yet, she's here.

She spins slowly, and her bright green eyes catch mine.

For a moment, she freezes like a deer in headlights. Then, a warm and teasing smile breaks through.

"You're supposed to be asleep," she says quietly as she goes to put a sleeping Luca down.

I step forward, unable to keep the smile off my own face.

"And miss this?" I gesture to her, to the twins, to the life I almost lost. "Not a chance."

She rolls her eyes as I stand before her, offering her my arms. "We never had the chance to dance at the opening night of the casino."

"I suppose we didn't."

Her eyes light up as she steps into me, hands clasping mine as I lead us in a gentle waltz around the room.

It's magical the way she tries to hush her laughter on behalf of the sleeping infants, the way the corners of her eyes crease with happiness as she presses herself into my chest.

Forever. This could be my forever.

As we slow down, I lean into her, unable to stop myself. Breath grazing over her ear. "Come to bed with me."

"Leon, I—"

"I love you. So much." My words fill the inches between us with something so precious. "You've done so well. You've looked after everyone. Please, let me look after you."

Her throat bobs as I lean in to press my lips to hers.

It's like a damn breaking.

It's been so long. There's never been enough time. Never been enough communication.

Now, we have all the time in the world.

It was only supposed to be chaste and convincing, but the kiss quickly becomes something else entirely. It's raw and desperate, filled with the longing of so many missed opportunities, so much time wasted.

Her lips part for me beautifully, and I stop wasting time. I lick into her mouth, entirely starved of the taste, already hungry for so much more.

"Fuck me," her voice wobbles, but the demand is absolute. "Leon, I need you so badly."

It's all the instruction I need. I take her in my arms, half dragging her along with me as she giggles behind me.

I have to stop on the stairs to kiss her again. She takes the step above mine so that I have to reach up to hold her there. Her arms wrap around my neck, and I lift her experimentally.

Yes, I can carry her. Thank fuck.

Her legs wrap around my waist, and I groan as she rubs herself against my straining cock. By the time we make it to the top of the stairs, all sense has evaporated from my mind.

I need her now. Right now.

Out of the corner of my eye, I see a mahogany console table. I don't think twice. The vases smash to the floor as I clear the surface. I ignore the stinging cuts of the ceramic against my ankles as I rest a wild-looking Mia on top of it.

"Leon. Leon," she groans as I pry her legs from my waist.

"Stay there. Good girl," I say as I tear my shirt from her body, leaving her beautiful and exposed to me like a piece of art. "I'm going to fuck you in every single room in this house."

To make my point abundantly clear, I unzip my pants and release myself in front of her.

Her pupils dilate as they always do when she takes in my size, reaching for me eagerly. But my fingers are already trailing down to her core, coating themselves in her wetness before stroking myself.

"Leon." My name on her lips is like a prayer.

I stalk forward, grabbing her chin with my hand, making a show of turning her face left and right so that she understands fully that I'm the one in control.

"I'm going to make you feel so fucking good. But you're going to have to trust me."

Whatever sound of agreement she makes is cut off when I dip my now rock-hard cock into her wetness.

She throws her head back in ecstasy as I bury myself within her. Her tight core takes my entire length to the hilt. The feeling of being inside of her is electric, and for a moment, I can't even feel the way her nails dig into my back.

"Move," she gasps at me.

"Say please," I tease, holding firm.

"I'm not going to beg."

I chuckle, knowing she will feel the vibrations inside her, too. "Yes, you are."

"Fuck," she groans. She leans into my neck to muffle the sound of her whimpers. "Please."

It's barely a whisper, but it's enough.

I'm not gentle, but neither is she. Over and over, I slam into her. The impact of our skin colliding fills the space with rhythmic thuds. The oil painting on the wall next to us crashes to the ground, but I don't care.

The feeling of her, the insatiable sounds she makes every time she takes me readily again and again, is the only thing I can focus on.

"Harder," she cries out, bracing herself on the light fittings.

Who am I to deny a request like that?

My thrusts turn into slower pounds. Her hips lift to meet me each time as I bury myself impossibly further into her. But it's not enough. I'm not close enough.

I lift her off the console in frustration, ignoring her protests as I carry her into the next room. The door to the bedroom opens with a slam, and I waste no time throwing her off me onto the bed.

I'm on her within seconds, planting kisses over every inch of exposed skin as I cradle her close.

She reaches for me, impatient as always, and I gladly slide back in.

We cling to each other this time, kissing and biting and mouthing at each other. I'm feral for something to claim while I pound into her over and over. Over and over. Over and over.

She wants it hard. She doesn't want me to hold back. I adjust her slightly to get the perfect angle, and her back obediently arches...

When Mia screams, it's with unbridled ecstasy. I can barely hold myself back as she rides through her orgasm.

My cock twitches inside of her. One more thrust, then another. Then.

"I love you."

I groan as I fall into my own ecstasy, riding the high of the feeling of her clenched around me. Her words echoing in my ears sound like the most beautiful thing I've ever heard.

"Say it again," I say, slowing down.

"I love you."

"Say it again," I say, holding her close.

"I love you."

I kiss her perfect lips and stare in wonder at her bright green eyes. Perfectly close. Perfect together.

"I love you, too."

EPILOGUE

Mia

Laughter floats through the open windows as I settle on the plush couch in Isabella's beautiful Bay Ridge living room.

Luca is on my lap, his tiny hands grasping for the toy dangling in front of him, while Liza is nestled in Isabella's arms, already dozing off with her thumb in her mouth.

Her daughter, Irina, sits on a soft blanket nearby, cooing at Cory as he babbles on at her with a confidence that he surely gets from Cassandra.

"I can't believe how big he is now, Cas," I marvel as the two-year-old pushes himself onto his feet and putters over to his mother.

Cas scoops Cory up with a proud smile. "He moves around so much I can barely keep track of him. I dread to think what it'll be like in your house when the twins reach this stage."

Isabella scoffs, her blonde hair tied back in a loose braid, starkly contrasting her sleek designer outfit. "What are you talking about? I'm never putting this one down."

She nuzzles into Liza's chin, staking her claim as the favorite aunty.

I tilt my head at her fondly. "Do you think you'll have another?"

Isabella laughs. "I think we have our hands full with these four, don't you? Besides, I think this is the perfect opportunity for us to open a bottle of wine. Can't do that if you're pregnant.

I can practically feel myself salivating. "Dear God, I haven't had a drink in almost a year. Please tell me you have tequila."

"Mia!" Cas lets out an undignified squeak.

I stick my tongue out at her. "I worked in a bar, Cas. Come on."

"I'll see what I can do." Isabella winks at me as she places Liza gently on the floor by a cooing Irina.

I settle back into the couch as Cas shakes her head, though I can see a smile tugging at the corner of her mouth.

From the next room, the low murmur of voices carries to us. The men are discussing business despite Leon insisting he wasn't going to talk shop tonight. But we all knew better.

"They'll be fine, you know?" Cas says, catching the direction of my gaze. "Together, they can take down anything."

I look at her and smile. "I know."

For the first time in a long time, I truly believe it.

Isabella returns a moment later carrying—bless her soul—three shots of clear tequila with matching wine glasses on a tray. A bottle of red wine is tucked haphazardly under her arm.

"Tadaa!"

"Issy, you are a godsend," I laugh as I take my shot when offered.

Cassandra leans over and taps her glass against mine.

"To survival," she says with a grin.

"To family," Isabella counters, lifting her glass.

"To the future," I say softly, my gaze drifting to our children.

We down the shots, and I try not to grimace as the liquid burns down my throat. I could have sworn this tasted better a year ago.

"Ugh!" Cas moans. "Never again. Issy, please pour me a glass of wine so I can at least pretend to be civilized when I drink."

I laugh as she continues to complain. The children around us are delighted by the warmth and love of our words, even if they don't quite understand them.

After a while, the low murmur of voices from the next room stops, replaced by the creak of the door opening.

I glance up just as Leon strides into the room, followed closely by Teo and Rocco. Leon's presence fills the space effortlessly, as it always does, his chocolate eyes scanning for me first.

When he finds me, his lips twitch in a small, reassuring smile, before he walks over to drop into the seat next to me. I curl into his warmth immediately, his arm stretching over my shoulder.

"Sorry for leaving," he murmurs as he kisses his temple.

Teo clears his throat, his hands clasped behind his back.

Despite his usual air of easy confidence, there's a weight to his expression tonight.

"Ladies," he begins, nodding at each of us, "I hope you're enjoying yourselves. I hate to interrupt, but we have an announcement to make."

Isabella raises a brow. "An announcement? Teo, why are you being so formal?"

On Teo's other side, Rocco barely suppresses a grin. "Just one more point of business, if you don't mind, Leon?"

Leon shrugs. "I think the ladies can handle it."

I elbow him in the ribs.

Teo clears his throat again. "The war with the Cartel has taken its toll on all of us. On our families, our businesses, our alliances. It's clear now that continuing as we always have isn't going to work. We need unity—true unity—if we're going to survive."

I snort loudly at this, drawing everyone's eyes. "I can't marry Leon again if that's what you're talking about."

"You could always divorce him," Cas teases, already on my wavelength.

Rocco rolls his eyes before stepping up to aid his friend in getting through his explanation.

"The Guild has been through a lot these few years, and the war against the Cartel has left our factions splintered. If it weren't for Leon's support, we wouldn't be standing here today."

A silence falls over the room, broken only by the soft murmurs of the babies.

"Leon's leadership in this war has been unmatched," Rocco continues. "His strategies, his determination, his sacrifices, they've kept us all afloat. Kept us alive."

Teo nods along with this before taking his lead. "That's

why Rocco and I have agreed: Leon will take over as the don of both the Guild and the Prince's Hand. Together, under one family."

My breath catches, and at my side, Leon looks...stunned.

His lips part as if to argue, but Teo raises a hand to stop him.

"Don't even start," Teo says. "You've earned this, Leon. Hell, you've *become* this. There's no one better suited to lead us through what's to come."

Rocco steps forward, his voice softer now. "You have my blessing, Leon. And my trust."

Leon looks at the two men, his jaw tight as he absorbs their words. Then, his gaze finds mine, lingering as if seeking my reaction.

I can only nod, my throat too tight to speak. Pride swells in my chest, mixed with a flicker of fear. But I know they are right. Leon was made for this.

"If this is what it takes to end this war and protect the people I care about," he says, his eyes still locked on mine, "then I'll do it."

Teo steps forward, clapping him on the back, his grin returning. "Good. Because we really weren't giving you the choice."

The room erupts in a mix of laughter and murmured congratulations, but my focus remains on Leon.

He truly glows under his new title of power. I can practically hear his mind running a thousand miles a second with the sheer number of possibilities it offers him. It's so terrifying and yet so perfectly right. I can't believe they never thought of it before.

"You sure okay with this?" he asks softly, his voice just for me.

And how can I deny this man a thing? "I'm sure. This is perfect."

He leans in, pressing a kiss to my forehead. "I couldn't do it without you."

I melt helplessly under his touch as the other men find their seats next to their respective wives.

"So, are you still going to call yourselves the Guild?" Cassandra says as she leans into her husband's side.

I watch as Teo and Leon exchange a glance. An unspoken conversation seems to pass between them before Teo shrugs. "I guess it would be the Prince's Guild now, wouldn't it?"

Isabella's eyes light up. "Oh, I love that!"

I laugh slightly at the insanity of it all. A year ago, these two factions were at each other's throats, fighting for dominance.

Now...now they exist together peacefully. The sounds of our children's laughter fill the air around us as news of the permanent union settles around the room.

For a long time after losing my father, I thought I was going to be alone.

But *this,* right here, is my family now.

"Hey," Leon whispers softly in my ear. "Do you think this is what happiness feels like?"

I turn to kiss him firmly on the lips. All mine. My husband.

"Yes. Yes, I do."

THE END

Read more from The Prince's Guild bestselling series, exclusive on Amazon:

Sin & Secrets: A Forced Proximity Mafia Romance
(Rocco & Cas)

Revenge & Ruin: An Enemies to Lovers Mafia Romance
(Teo & Isabella)

Deception & Desire: An Arranged Marriage Mafia Romance
(Leon & Mia)

Obsession & Oath: A Forbidden Bodyguard Mafia Romance
(Dante & Carmen)